MIDLife

HARRY PANTS

SILKY OAK PRESS

Australia

This first edition published 2013
by Silky Oak Press
ABN 45 969 162 506
www.silkyoakpress.com.au

Written by Harry
Edited by Dave
Proofread by Greg
Book Design by Ron
Cover Design by Juliette
Typeset in Adobe Garamond Pro 12/17

ISBN 978 0 9923928 0 2

This story is written in Australian English

For my Dad,
who knew how to love, and to laugh.

The Chapters

1
Choking Man Blue

SOMETHING WAS DIFFERENT, and I couldn't quite put my finger on it. Well, I could have, but to do so would be the sort of putting your finger on something that usually leads to sex or trouble. Which is often the same thing. Not that I really remembered.

You see, the thing I couldn't quite put my finger on — or could have if I was still young enough, energetic enough or simply bothered enough to find out which of the possibilities it might lead to — was my wife's left breast.

It was, for the sake of a better word, out. And when I say out, I don't mean out as in out of bounds, or out of play, or out of fashion, but out as in … well … okay, I'll just tell you. I'll give it to you straight. Up here, not too far below chin level, standing proudly in the breeze covered in nothing but fake tan, was the breast, and down there somewhere below it, attempting to garner attention only by its garish blue colour and occasional billowing proximity to the nipple, was the part of the dress connected to the thin strap whose job it was to hold the dress up, thereby preserving what little modesty my lovely wife still retained.

Hmmm. That's different, I thought.

Usually, ever since she started carrying on about how *old* she feels, and how *boring* life is, and how we really need to *spice things up*, and ever since she started the *just having a little work done* obsession — which of course included a rather large and strangely firm pair of new breasts that are *worth every cent* — the usual place for the breasts, including the left one, had been inside the comfortable, professionally fitted home of some *also worth every cent* brassieres, which were in turn well covered with some *understated* designer label and *beautifully cut* clothing. Also new most days.

Yet there we were, Friday night, ten minutes to seven, which is to say ten minutes to guests due for dinner, and most of the *perfectly pert yet pendulously bulbous* left breast leapt out of its *so Parisienne* evening dress to greet me as I arrived home from work.

Now don't get me wrong, I'm not complaining. As I said, it was just different. Perhaps I should have seen all this coming — of course there were clues, aren't there always? But really, I've never been the sort of man for clues, or games, or jigsaws or scrabble or cryptic crosswords for that matter.

I was young once of course, but I never was any good at the dating game, the rituals that go with that territory, and to be truthful — and I will be, although that too is hardly fashionable now in the twenty-first century—I was a 20 year old virgin when I met Masey, and a 21 year old virgin when I married her. I'd never slept with another woman, which is not to say I hadn't noticed any that made me think about it, or even thought about how that might feel. But really, they'd been 31 pretty good years, and I had nothing to complain about. I was already in the management program of a leading food supply company when I met her, and I'd continued to rise through the ranks, all the way to National Supply Manager. I was great at what I did, had been in the top job for the past twelve years, and made enough money for us to live in a great house in a leafy suburb. Enough in fact, that she'd never had to do a day of paid work in her life.

She'd been a good mum by most standards, served on committees at James's school, helped out charitable causes, and led a good and fulfilling life. She was a fine citizen with a great sense of self worth and a hint of nipple visible along with most of a *perfectly pert yet pendulously bulbous* left breast—well, that's what they'd called it in the catalogue. Regardless, it was a breast that no longer did anything for me, not that I could have told her that, but really, I loved the one, well the two to be technically correct, that were there before, her natural breasts, and, well, these unbouncy mounds of flesh-covered plastic may defy gravity, but they're just not really a part of Masey are they?

There. I said it. Not to her, obviously, but at least to you. And now, depending on your personal views, you'll probably be annoyed, or not, most likely the former, but I can't help it. And anyway, she'd never actually cared what I thought. She hadn't listened when I told her she was beautiful just the way she was, and she'd said I was just being cheap. So, the dilemma I now faced was whether to immediately mention that she had forgotten to wear a bra and her perfectly built, gravity-defying skin-covered plastic mid-life crisis averting left breast was on display for all to see — or to wait until the guests arrived and see if they brought it to her attention, or perhaps just ignored the whole thing and pretended it wasn't happening, or…

'What's with the crazy-eyes, Wallace?' she said.

'Hello Darling, your magnificent new breast is showing, just so you know.'

'Nonsense Wallace. Don't be such a prude, it's just a little skin.'

'Actually Dear, it's several magnificently bulbous acres of skin, not to mention a rather perfectly pointed point, shouldn't you be wearing a bra with that lovely blue dress? What's the name of that colour? Choking Man Blue perhaps. Lovely, just lovely. You look stunning, by the way. As always.'

'Oh, you're such an exaggerator Wallace, really you are. Now quickly run upstairs, shower and dress. I've laid out

4

your clothes for you, tonight will be quite special and I won't have you stuffing it all up ... well run along.'

That was my first clue, though in hindsight I suppose it should have been about my thirtieth. Or so.

2

Don't Talk to the Underpants

As ALWAYS, I did as I was told and made my way upstairs
to ready myself for yet another Friday night dinner party.
We used to have these perhaps once a month, but recently
it'd been every Friday and Saturday night, unless we'd
been invited to some other *lovely home* or restaurant for
fine dining and *intelligent conversation*.

I thought about all this as I showered, and truth be
known, I'd have been happier to be allowed to come
home and have a quiet night in, just the two of us, or
even alone, but those options were no longer available.
My social butterfly had seen to that. I suppose one must
get all the value one can out of one's new appearance
given the cost of it, both financial and, as I'd heard so
many times lately, *the pain I go through to look attractive
for you Wallace.*

Yes Dear. Thank you Darling. You look wonderful.
And other platitudes.

Actually, she looked very beautiful indeed before the
tummy tuck and the *breast augmentation* and the *lipo* and
the *just a teensy brow lift.* But now she just looked less like

herself, which I found silly, because herself had been a very fine way to look before she'd started meddling with it.

So there on the bed was my outfit for the evening. A ridiculously shiny suit, whiter than white shirt and a fat grey tie. And leather underpants.

Okay, I thought again ... That's different.

'Excuse me Masey,' I called from the top of the stairs, 'but some strange seventies disco freak has stolen my clothes and left his on our bed.'

'You're not amusing Wallace. Hurry. They'll be here any minute. And behave yourself. You will not embarrass me. We're going to have a wonderful time tonight.'

'Is it fancy dress Dear? And do the underpants go on the outside li...'

'Wallace! Shut up and dress. You must look your best for Derek and Cynthia.'

'Who the hell are Derek and Cynthia?' I asked, folding myself into the satin suit while contemplating the shiniest and widest tie I'd ever seen.

'Do you NEVER listen to me Wallace? I told you all about this. Cynthia is my yoga instructor. Her husband made his money in computer software. Don't worry, you're going to adore them. Trust me Darling, this will be a night you'll remember for a very long time.'

'What a pity,' I told the tie. 'I was hoping this was all a dream and I'd forget it before I awoke.' I refused to talk to the underpants, and left them on the bed to get lonely. I almost wished I were them.

3
A Lovely Soft Rope

WE FOUR overdressed seventies types stood around in the formal lounge room with our glasses of *eighteen year old scotch*, making small talk about the *eclectic modern art* on the walls and expressing admiration for each other's outfits. The Cynthia woman was attractive in her way, but unfortunately her way was the same way Masey had gone of late, that is to say a face that didn't quite manage the shape of a smile when she wanted it to and large fake breasts that were perilously close to jumping out of their bright red low-cut evening dress and knocking someone's eye out.

And Derek—well, what could one say about Derek? It seemed that Derek too was under strict orders regarding his clothing. Like myself he was buttoned down into a shimmering suit, with fat grey tie to match. We were as two peas in a pod, except that the pea that arrived on Cynthia's arm had long and *luscious hair, simply divine Darling*.

'Oh, you must feel how soft it is', said Cynthia. 'It's like a lovely soft rope,' and the three of them giggled like the silliest of schoolgirls.

How strange it was, to watch my wife's hand guided onto another man's long black ponytail by another woman, to sense a thing I was much too slow to have seen, to wonder if my mind was playing tricks, or if I was just tired. It was Friday after all, perhaps I'd been overdoing work a little, or was coming down with something—or was it just the surreal quality of the clothing, its other-worldness, the scotch, the...

'Wallace Dear, you *simply must* feel Derek's ponytail, it's wonderful.'

'Oh yes,' agreed Cynthia, seizing the opportunity to advance on me, 'Do you like to touch silky soft things Wallace?'

I felt off kilter again—Cynthia's arm snaking around me; her hand gripping my own; her bullying breasts push-ing against my back as her insistent crotch wrapped around my leg—the whole thing seemingly designed to move me toward her husband and his *mesmerising* length of rope-like hair.

The me that is me floated back to the surface just before she managed to guide my hand onto the offered ponytail, and I used my free hand to undo her grip and break away.

'Thanks anyway,' I said. 'I'm trying to cut down. Refill anyone?'

'What lovely strong hands you have Wallace,' said Cyn-thia. Then quietly, smoothing my tie and leaning in so our lips and noses almost touched, 'We must put them to better use later.'

I was aware of how unconvincing my smile was. I felt myself blushing, and was suddenly quite caught up in the feeling I was being had in some way, but not quite sure just which way that might have been. Had Derek and Masey heard what was said? They were just a few feet away, laughing, but paying no attention to us at all. In fact, they appeared to be quite wrapped up in their own private little world. Once again, I had that feeling I was falling behind, too slow for my life as it unfolded before me, and I tried to set things right by throwing back a rather large shot of lovely Laphroaig scotch, pouring myself another, and wondering aloud what might be for dinner.

'Oh Wallace,' said Masey. 'You really must pay more attention when I speak to you. Dinner is being delivered, we're having Thai.'

As if on cue the doorbell went ding dong ding dong, and I seized the opportunity to escape what had become quite the bewildering situation.

Having paid an even $150 for $111 worth of Thai food—*No no, not allowed carry change*—I retreated to the kitchen for some thinking time while I arranged the various dishes into proper serving bowls, which Masey had preheated in the oven. We disliked fast food containers. We disliked many things. I was often told which things we disliked. Naturally, my new-found solitude didn't last. Cynthia joined me in the kitchen, supposedly sent by Masey to help, as Derek was in the middle of 'a hilarious story that was absolutely and positively too wonderful to interrupt.'

'Why don't you go back and hear the story Cynthia? I have this under control, really.'

'I've heard it several times before. It's his go-to story for impressing the girls he plans to sleep with. I'm much more interested in you, Wallace.' This while once again showing more than a passing interest in my ridiculous tie, patting it, running her fingers from the top to the bottom of it, then wrapping it around the back of her neck and saying, 'Oh dear Wallace, I do believe you've caught me. The question is, what do you plan to do with me now?'

'Umm … well, perhaps I'll get you to help me carry the food to the dining room then. Can't have it getting cold, can we?'

Her eyes fluttered movie star style, and she laughed, effectively managing to rub her nose, cheek, breasts and pubis against me all at once, before placing my tie very carefully back where it belonged, straightening its knot, and telling me, 'You're funny Wallace. I think we're going to have a lovely time together, you and I. Lead the way to the dining room, kind sir. We'll continue this discussion later, shall we?'

Obviously, I'd had too much scotch. Or not enough. Or this was not actually happening, or it was happening, but to someone else, and I'd been abducted by aliens and dropped back into the wrong body.

Then again, I didn't feel probed... although the way Cynthia looked at me as we picked up the bowls of pad thai and prawn green curry and whatever the hell else $111 plus a $39 tip buys, it seemed that probing may well have been on the agenda for later. Hmmm, I thought, perhaps I'm still on the spaceship, and Cynthia and Derek are the...

'There you are, you naughty pair,' said Derek, 'I was beginning to wonder if you'd skipped dinner and gone straight to dessert without us. My wife is quite delicious, wouldn't you agree Wallace? But of course, you're used to that.'

This last comment he made while looking at Masey as if she was food, and he was hungry. Which of course he was supposed to be, it being dinner time and everything, but, again, the whole thing was becoming much more difficult to...

'I'm quite sure Wallace can be talked into something sweet after dinner, can't you Wallace?'

'Well, Cynthia, I am trying to watch my weight, and...'

'Such a shy boy, aren't you? We must teach him some new tricks Masey dear, don't you agree?'

'Well, he's not very smart Cyn darling, but he's quite the obedient one. Perhaps we'll buy him a lovely leather collar.'

I reached for the scotch as they all cracked up laughing at their *tremendously amusing* jokes. And I continued to reach for it several more times during dinner.

4

Bannister, Horse, Banana

OKAY, FIRSTLY, I'd just like to say, in my own defence, that I don't usually have more than three drinks on any given night, and am in fact, not terribly good at drinking.

And secondly, I'd like to stress what I said firstly.

So, there may be a few gaps here, but what I do remember is that on this particular evening, in our comfortable home in our upper-class suburb, it seemed to be a good idea, whenever I didn't quite understand what was going on, to busy myself pretending I was busy pouring and drinking scotch. And that at some point I realised that I'd gotten rather too good at pretending, or perhaps less good at pretending and more good at actually drinking the scotch. And that at some other point a lot of things became even less clear than they had been, and I may or may not have done some things I wouldn't normally do.

The possible events of the evening can be divided into two main categories. Category One I'll call flashes of memory. These may not be reliable. Certainly one of them involved an extremely tall, thin horse that wore red high heels and screeched like a black cockatoo. This rather angry horse began kicking me repeatedly in and around the groin area before galloping into my house and slamming the front door behind it. While this particular memory seems unlikely, the various pains and swellings around my groin area for the following few days seemed to bear witness to the possibility, however I could not swear to it in a court of law.

Other flashes of memory in this possibly unreliable category include: Masey meowing whilst wearing Derek's ponytail as a collar; me apologising to Cynthia for getting her hair wet when I accidentally spilled my drink into my lap; Cynthia and Masey both attempting to clean my pants with their tongues at the same time; Masey complaining that I hadn't worn the leather underpants; Derek's leather underpants having metal studs on them; Cynthia and Masey kissing each other while Derek attempted to grind the studs off his underpants by rubbing them against the bannisters; me drowning in a sea of enormously bulbous yet unforgiving breasts; Masey hitting me over the head because I couldn't stop laughing at Derek's short, fat and somewhat misshapen penis; Cynthia offering me the last of the scotch then pouring it over her quite naked body; me bursting into my own bedroom to see Derek tying Masey to the bed with the fat grey ties Derek and I had been wearing until various parts of our clothing had fallen off; Cynthia trying to calm me down in the front yard as I attempted to use a banana to unlock my car door; me falling into the bushes that line our driveway; me telling the tall thin horse that was standing over me that it seemed to have a remarkably cute bald rat between its legs; and of course the aforementioned kicking, pain, etcetera, in and around my groin area.

As so few of these rather fuzzy memories bear any resemblance whatsoever to anything that had happened in the previous 51 years of my life, I must cast them aside as extremely unlikely, and put it down to a bad pad thai coupled with perhaps thirty or so too many glasses of scotch, and try Category Two in an attempt to reconstruct the events of the evening based on photographic evidence, some of which I found on my phone, and some of which was sent to me via my phone by Masey later the following day.

This photographic evidence consisted of:

Exhibit A: A somewhat blurred shot of what could be Masey and Cynthia with their tongues down each other's throats, and what is quite likely Derek standing in close proximity to the bannisters behind them.

Exhibit B: Something that may well be my chin and bottom lip amidst what appears to be a rolling sea of bulbous flesh, including either two quite different looking nipples and the point of a tongue, or possibly a third somewhat blurred nipple.

And Exhibit C: Courtesy of a picture message from Masey's phone the following morning: Masey's lips and tongue in close proximity to something that looked like a remarkably cute bald rat, with the hem of a striking red dress floating above it.

I suppose these various pieces of evidence could be enough to begin to compile a somewhat factual account of the evening in question. But I needed more. Obviously, something was missing. An independent processor of thoughts and evidence.

And that was where Bruce came in.

5
A Good Whipping

I WOKE on the morning after the night in question to find myself being viciously bitten on the bare behind by an extremely loud, aggressive, and angry animal. The pain was excruciating, my head almost exploding at the sound of the screams, and continuing to pound long after I realised the screams were coming from me and somehow managing to make them stop.

'Fuck me fucken drunk, waddaya doing in there ya mad bastard?' asked a rather too loud voice as the noise of the screaming animal subsided. 'I coulda cut ya tackle off with me whippy ya mad fuck! Where's ya clothes mate? Jeez, yer fucken bleedin. Do the garden good anyways.'

The lawnmower man put his whipper snipper aside, took off his shirt and threw it at me.

'Ya wanna cover up your business and explain to me what you're doing lying there in the bushes? Lucky you're face down, I woulda cut yer tadger off. Who the fuck are you anyways?' he asked as if he owned the place.

The sun beat down on my pounding head and I wished I had more of a religious belief so I could ask whichever god I worshipped to kill me now, but pleasant as that particular thought was, it was getting me nowhere. The fresh whipper snipper cuts to my rump competed with the many other pains in my body, and a vision of a red shoe repeatedly moving at lightning speed toward my naked scrotum flashed into the forefront of my bewildered brain. I looked up at my lawnmower man and realised I'd never met him, but between my dry mouth and the pain and the visions of the previous evening flashing through what was left of my mind, I was finding it somewhat difficult to introduce myself.

I covered my poor bruised meat and potatoes with Lawnmower Man's shirt with one hand, and allowed him to help me to my feet with the other. The sun was high enough in the sky that I remembered it was Saturday, and therefore I should have been at work. That was when I noticed an unpeeled banana with a squashed end on the ground beside my car door.

'Yawda MowaMan,' I managed to croak.

'No shit Sherlock,' he replied. 'And who the fuck might you be?'

'Wolwess Head,' I replied. 'Wo … Wol … Ffuck.'

'No shit? Been mowin yer place for a year and never met you. And here you are. Bleedin from the arse at the end of me whipper snipper. This ain't my fault mate. What the fuck were you thinkin? Sleepin naked in the fucken bushes, for shit's sake. Fucken mad. And I thought all you rich pricks round here was the conservative types. Best get you inside so you can wash up and get some clothes on I reckon.'

He was right, of course. We rich pricks around here definitely were the conservative types. Whatever had happened here last night, and indeed was happening now, was the most action our perfectly manicured, quietly conservative street had seen in many a year. I could feel all the accusing eyes on me, peering from behind richly brocaded curtains as I walked to my door, an embarrassing spectacle to be talked about in hushed tones for years to come.

Remembering a flash of the night before, I noticed Derek and Cynthia's car was gone, and wondered what Masey would think of me bleeding on the *calacatta marble* floor as Lawnmower Man helped me through the front door. He brought me some water from the kitchen as I lay in a crumpled bleeding heap on the *full-grain Italian leather lounge.*

'Jeez mate, you look a bit worse for wear. Big night?' He laughed, but even though every sound he made echoed like a Tibetan gong through every shattered fibre of my being, I could tell he wasn't being unkind. He was different to the people I knew.

'Are you gonna be right, mate?' he asked. 'I gotta finish the lawn, but you still don't look the best. Hate to have you pass out and smack your head on the tiles or something.'

'Can you walk up the stairs there, knock on the second door to the right and call Masey please?' It occurred to me that it couldn't be a good idea to send a man as tall and muscular and good-looking as this one to your wife's bedroom, but given the events of the night before, I wondered if that may have been like closing the gate after the horse had bolted.

'No worries mate. Wally is it? No worries Wal, I'll go wake her up for you.'

He was gone just long enough for my head to pound sixteen times, at which point he announced, 'She ain't there Wal. Doors are all open, there's no-one here but us. She left you a note on the mirror though I reckon. Lipstick I hope... same colour as what you're drippin onto the floor there. "Fuck You Limp Dick" the note says. Real big too. Upset the little woman did you mate?'

I groaned and stretched out on the leather lounge, worrying what she'd say about the blood I was dripping and hoping my wounds might prove fatal, and preferably sooner rather than later.

Lawnmower Man brought me some more water.

'Thank you,' I said. 'What's your name?'

'Bruce mate. It's nice to meet ya Wally. Sorry about your arse.'

'My head hurts. What a night. I can't really remember much.'

'Yeah, no good the grog. I used to drink a bit, but not any more. You should give that up mate, you look shockin.'

'Thanks. I don't usually drink much. It's just … these people were here … these weird … oh my head.'

'They reckon bacon and eggs are the go. For a hangover I mean. Got any? Can't just watch you suffer can I?'

'Umm. Maybe. Have a look. Bruce is it? Have a look please Bruce. Thanks.'

So the lawnmower man went to the kitchen, made a huge spattery mess cooking bacon and eggs, burned some toast, set off the smoke alarms, which set off my head alarms, and brought me a huge pile of bacon and eggs, toast with more butter than I've ever seen melting all over the plate, and a beautiful cup of sugary coffee. Twenty minutes later, I felt almost human again.

So we sat and talked and tried to piece the previous night together, and everything I told him set him off laughing again, then he had a brainstorm and said, 'Check your phone. Photos mate!'

And there they were. Firstly, Exhibit A, and Bruce yelled 'Wowee, lezzo action.' Then followed Exhibit B, and Bruce said, 'You lucky bastard, look at THAT for a tittie-bath,' and even I laughed at that one.

I sent a message to Masey:

**Where are you Dear? And what happened
last night?**

She immediately sent one back.

Well, actually what she sent back was a picture message, and because the photo was side on I didn't quite see what it was, so I said, 'What the fuck is that?'

Bruce looked over my shoulder and started cracking up and said, 'Never seen one before mate? What do they teach you richies in them private schools anyway? Looks like a wild pussy with a tongue chasin it if you ask me.'

So I turned it side on and there it was — the remarkably cute bald rat, with Masey's tongue an inch away from it, and I pressed the button so the message scrolled down and it said

**This is what happened. And by the way
I'm leaving you. Derek Cyn and I going
to Bali. Go fuck yourself Mr Prude.**

6
Someone Else's Life

'WELL, WOZZA, looks like you just bought yourself a whole paddock full of dog shit to mow.'

'She'll calm down,' I said. Maybe I said it wrong, but somehow I failed to convince me.

'Course she will mate. You know her better than I do. Reckon she calls you a limpdick in big red letters on the hallway mirror and sends you photos of herself with her tongue gettin ready to clean out some woman's pleasure-palace every Saturday. Just before she runs off to Bali with a couple of buddies she met at the local knitting club mate. Normal everyday Saturday for you I reckon. Best start cleaning that blood up mate. Hate to get any on your divorce papers.'

Oh god, I thought. 'Oh god' I said.

It didn't help. I wondered if it might have been the whole atheism thing. Still, even we atheists had our crosses to bear. Or should that have been bare? Whatever it was, I still felt like I'd been in fights with several rats, horses, and whipper snippers, and as I quite suddenly felt an oppressive weight on me, I realised it wasn't a cross at all, but rather divorce lawyers sensing my blood.

Bruce looked around at the trappings of our upper middle class life, all the things that were supposedly making us happy, looked at me with genuine pity in his face, and shook his head. 'Gonna be expensive mate. Best thing I can tell you ... don't let it destroy you. It's only money. Some blokes let it become more, and never get over it. It's only money.'

'She'll be back. Really. It's just a one-off. We're happily married, truly.'

'Okay Wally. Sure you are,' he said. 'Who are you trying to convince mate? I'm just the bloke who mows the lawn.'

'Are you married Bruce?'

'Not any more, mate. Ten years was enough. For her as well as me. Marriage is like a garden I reckon. After a while, no matter what you do, it's all too much work for not enough reward. One day you're pulling out the same weeds you pulled out last month, or trimming the low branches off the same tree you trimmed them off last year, and you start thinking about why you're doing it, and you can't remember why you started to in the first place. Why you planted that particular tree, or chose that type of grass for the lawn, or why you even bothered with having a garden at all, cos the fact is, you haven't sat your arse down out there and looked around and enjoyed it in years anyway. You was just going through the motions, doing what you did cos it's what people do, what's expected of you, so you just keep right on doing it. When my missus fucked off, I realised I was living someone else's life, and I never even knew who I was. So … question is, who are you Wally?'

'Well, that's easy,' I said. 'I'm me. I'm Wallace Head, National Supply Manager of one of the biggest food supply chains in the world. I'm a husband and a father. I own a beautiful home and drive a lovely new car and have a very comfortable life indeed. I'm…I…'

There was nothing else to say. Each sentence that came out of me felt impotent, empty as this house had been since the day James left for New York four years ago. I had no idea who I was or where I'd left me behind. All this … stuff … these fancy tiles and the slick modern furniture and the silly art on the walls, all of it just things I didn't choose, didn't like, didn't care enough to do anything more than pay for.

And I thought of Masey … my beautiful Masey … the one thing I actually did choose, did bother to want and to chase and to make plans to have in my life. She was gone, and maybe this mad mowing guy was right — maybe marriage is like a garden, but maybe I never did anything else after planting the seeds, and all this plastic surgery and renovations to the house and the new car and these stupid erotic books she's been asking me to read, and these stupid pretentious friends she keeps inviting to dinner, maybe all of it's just a…

'Well I better go finish your lawn,' said Bruce. 'Feel free to give us a call if you wanna talk mate.'

7

You Said You Were A Large Pumpkin

I THOUGHT she'd come back later that day. She didn't.

I thought she'd come back the next day. Instead of going to work I stayed home to wait for her. She didn't turn up. I tried her number. She didn't answer. Seventeen times.

I tried drinking again. It made my head hurt, and she still didn't come home.

Every time the phone rang I assumed it was Masey, calling to apologise, to tell me how much she loved me, begging to be forgiven, wanting to come home.

It never was. It was always someone from work, so I never answered, except for once when it was a private number, which had to be Masey, in trouble and desperate. But it wasn't her—it was a telemarketer calling from India or Punchbowl or Gulargambone or somewhere, one of those sorts of places where telemarketer sorts of people must live and work. Everyone knows telemarketers only call at dinner time, so I realised it must be dinner time, and I remembered I'd been forgetting to eat.

I ordered pizza. Eventually it arrived, and I paid fifty dollars for a twenty-two dollar pizza.

'I sorry Missa, no allowed carry change.' He looked suspiciously like the Thai delivery guy.

The pizza was cold. I ate one slice and drank the last two beers.

The next morning, at eleven-thirty-two, I woke up because the doorbell was going ding dong ding dong, ding dong ding dong. She must have lost her keys. I dragged myself off the lounge, threw a cushion over the bloodstain I'd forgotten to clean, walked over and opened the door, ready to read her the riot act for making me worry this way.

Or have wild yet tender make-up sex.

Or read her the riot act while having wild yet tender make-up sex.

It was going to be great. We hadn't had sex for a really long time.

I opened the door. It was two rather small policemen. Well, one was a woman, but the other had no excuse. What's with this shrinking police force anyway? Used to be the mere sight of the...

'Wallace Head?' asked the woman.

'No, I'm a large pumpkin. Who else would I be?'

'You might be a burglar who's killed Wallace Head and

decided to live in his house and wear his exceedingly silly pyjamas,' said the woman.

The Tiny Officer Man smirked. Small man syndrome probably.

'Why would I do that? I'm a perfectly decent man. I never kill anybody. And what's wrong with my pyjamas? And where's my wife? What's happened to her?'

'We don't know anything about your wife sir. Perhaps she's left you for someone who doesn't have little toy trains on their pyjamas,' said the rather rude little woman.

'Well why aren't you out there looking for her, instead of harassing innocent citizens about their pyjamas? And they're not toys. This one's the Ghan, and this one's the Orient Express, and this one's the…'

'We're here to find Wallace Head, sir. He's been reported missing. Hasn't been to work for days, and doesn't answer his phone. Very unlike him. Have you seen him?'

'What do you mean, have I seen him? I AM him. I told you so already. What's all this about?'

'No you didn't sir. You told us you were a pumpkin,' she said.

'A large pumpkin,' the Tiny Officer Man corrected her, looking up from his notebook.

'Thank you Officer Large,' she said. 'A large pumpkin.'

'Well of course I'm not a … What's wrong with you people?'

'So are you saying you lied to us sir?' she said, taking a small notebook from her pocket. 'That's a very serious offence.'

Obviously the notebook police.

'Look. Where is my wife? I am Wallace Head, and my wife is missing, why don't you go and find her?'

'Have you reported her missing sir?'

'Well, not exactly,' I said. 'She's only been gone a few days.'

'This is beginning to sound very serious sir. And rather suspicious actually. I must warn you, that you are not obliged to say or do anything, but anything you…'

'For fuck's sake, what is wrong with you people? Are you even really police officers? I…'

*

I woke up. I was bleeding on the lounge again. Lady Policeman was inspecting the art, and Tiny Officer Man was coming back from the kitchen, wiping his truncheon with a tea-towel.

'Ah, you're awake,' he said, throwing me the tea-towel. 'You'd better put this on your head. You're getting blood on your wife's lounge.'

'You hit me,' I said.

'Calm down sir, you're obviously deluded. You were

babbling about your wife, then you fainted. You must have hit your head when you fell. Now let's clear this little mess up shall we? Firstly, we're here because you were reported missing by the people you work with. Despite you being less than co-operative, we've managed to ascertain your identity by good police work. No need to thank us. It's what we do.'

He paused, waiting for me to thank him. I didn't.

'Firstly, Mister Head...'

'Don't you mean secondly?' I enquired. 'Wasn't firstly the bit about me being reported missing?'

He started to raise his truncheon. Apparently small police officers hate to appear stupid as well as tiny. Luckily for my head the doorbell went ding dong ding dong, ding dong ding dong. It saved me from fainting and hitting my head on the floor again.

'Don't get up, I'll get it,' said Lady Policeman, as she walked across the room, picking up my wallet from the coffee table as she went. Tiny Officer Man stood there, glaring at me as he tapped his small hand ever so gently with his large truncheon. I wondered if he realised the implications of a tiny man softly beating his depressingly small hand with his overcompensatingly large truncheon, in a rhythm somewhat similar to that of a dog's hind leg hitting the floor as it... It was no way to be thinking about the Police Force, so I let it go.

It was then I noticed some talking and laughing, and Lady Policeman came back into the room with some containers of Thai food. The smell of it made my nuts hurt.

'We decided to accept your generous offer to eat lunch while we interview you Mister Head,' she said. 'The food was $104, but he had no change, so I had to take three fifties from your wallet to pay him.'

'How very generous of you,' I told her, with all the sarcasm a man pressing a blood-soaked tea-towel against a deep wound in his skull can manage.

'Don't mention it sir,' she said.

'Yeah,' Tiny Policeman added, raising his truncheon again. 'Seriously. DON'T mention it.'

And so they talked and questioned and ate, and I lay on the lounge bleeding into my tea-towel and answering their questions, and the upshot of it all was that they decided I was undoubtedly too stupid to have murdered my wife, that I was such an insufferable bore that it was surprising she hadn't left me years earlier, and that the only crimes committed here had been my crime against fashion by wearing the particular pyjamas I had on.

Then they left, taking the leftover Thai food with them.

8
Well, It Felt Like a Tail

I GROVELLED around the house for a few more days, but nobody called or visited, not even in my dreams. It had been a week since Masey had left, and I hadn't been out of the house. Problem was, I'd started eating again, but quickly ran out of food, and my wallet was empty. Masey had taken the credit cards.

There was nothing else for it. I'd have to go to the bank. I decided to shower. I'd avoided mirrors for a week, mostly just lying on the bloody lounge and watching TV, and was actually quite interested in what I saw in the mirror, now that I actually looked. It wasn't me. I had the beginnings of a pretty decent beard, something I'd never had before, and must admit I quite liked. I had a large scab disappearing from my forehead into my hairline.

Never fuck with a tiny policeman.

I quite liked the look of it though. I looked like ... a man.

I considered not showering for a second, thought maybe I'd just go with the man smell, throw on some jeans and a T-shirt, but the stench that attacked me when I took off my pyjamas was enough to send me scurrying to the shower.

I scrubbed myself all over, twice—jerked off onto the handpainted tile of a scantily clad nymphette, once—and shaved, not at all. It was almost a comfort, Masey's voice in my head, whinging and whining and bitching, *you can't go out looking like that, what will people think, we have an image to uphold, people expect...*

'FAAAAAAAAAAAARRRRRK.'

What a pretentious bitch she could be. Maybe I was better off without her. God I missed her.

I dressed in clothes. I drove to the bank. I went into the bank. It was boring there. The people working in the bank were nice to me, as if they knew they should feel sorry for me, a downtrodden husband, possibly a drunk, probably soon to have divorce lawyers after his blood, a police brutality victim, a man unable to go to his job because of shame and—well, truth be told, mostly a lack of desire to tell anyone why I'd stopped going to work.

Why had I stopped going to work? I'd always enjoyed work. Not in the way one might enjoy, say, driving a race car on a track, or finding a new bicycle under the tree on Christmas morning when you were seven, or being dipped in chocolate, wrapped in a red ribbon, and delivered to Angelina Jolie for dessert. But, you know, like you might enjoy, say, getting up very early six or seven days a week, fifty weeks a year, showering and shaving and buttoning yourself into a boring suit, battling your way through the traffic, spending all day dealing with all sorts of stupid problems, trying to make a few arse-holes happy no matter how many other people were made unhappy, staying back late, driving home again, being greeted with a few put-downs by a pretentious woman who'd spent the day wasting the money you earned, and trying to get some sleep before doing it all over again the next day.

These poor arse-holes in the bank didn't know a thing. I was the one better off. I may have had a weeping head wound, blood on my T-shirt and still been on the smelly side of what passes as twenty-first century society's convention, but I was free.

Free.

Honest.

I got my money, bought some food, and drove home with my beard itching my face and my tail between my legs. Well, it felt like a tail…

2
Dustin Hoffman Tells a Dirty Story

I DROVE HOME. I parked the car in the garage. I took the groceries inside. I decided to make a sandwich. There wasn't any bread. But I could get around any challenge that life could throw at me. I was free and proud of it.

I took out the cheese and the sliced ham I'd bought. I took three slices of cheese from their plastic wrappers and placed them on the kitchen bench-top. I took three slices of ham and put them next to the cheese. I removed the plastic from another slice of cheese and placed it on top of a slice of ham. I took another slice of ham and placed that on top of the cheese. I now had a cheese sandwich on ham-bread. I ate it. Quite satisfying. I was a chef.

I unwrapped the other two slices of cheese. This was going great. I placed the remaining slice of ham on top of one slice of cheese, then the other slice of cheese on top of that. Fantastic. A ham sandwich on cheese-bread. I went to pick it up to eat it, but the bottom slice of cheese stuck to the stainless steel bench-top and the rest of the sandwich fell off the bench onto my pants, my shoes, and the floor. I picked a lot of it up, scraped the cheese slice off the bench-top with a rather manky-looking teaspoon, scrunched it all into a ball in my hand so it stayed together, and invented the cheese and ham squelch. Delicious. Except for the bits of dirt and some hair from the floor, but nothing's perfect first time, right? Next time I'll know to clean the floor before attempting to prepare such extraordinarily complex culinary delights.

So, I've eaten. And shopped. Now what? I could have a sleep. Flog the log again maybe? Hmmm. This man of leisure thing's hard work.

I decided to try calling Masey again. What would I say though? Hi Masey, just checking how you are. I don't go to work any more, and I'm growing a beard, oh, and working on my cooking skills. You should come home for dinner sometimes.

Clearly, I was confused. This being your own man thing wasn't as easy as it looked. What I needed was a mentor. What I needed was someone who'd been through this shit before, who'd survived it, who was relatively happy and…

What I needed was my lawn-mowing man!

I decided to look for his number. Times gone by, it would have been right beside the phone, on a little thing called a telephone table, in a little book called a rolodex, written down in pen or pencil along with every other phone number you'd ever need. And the phone was attached to the wall, so you always knew where it was.

But these are modern times, when the world is so effi-cient we have everyone's number at the touch of a fucking screen, and the screen is some-fucking-where-else, a tiny thing you first have to locate. I eventually found my phone in the car, but Bruce's number wasn't in it. I didn't know where to look after that. Was it true? Was I really so useless I couldn't find a phone number if it wasn't in my own phone?

I turned on the computer to do an internet search. I didn't know his last name. A Google search for Bruce found 455 million results. I narrowed the search by adding lawnmower. Now I was making progress. Only 1,480,000 results. I was hot on the trail.

The first result was for Bruce's Lawn Mowing, but it was in the wrong state. Next was Bruce's Lawn Mower Shop, but it was in the wrong country. I watched a you-tube video called Monty Python – Bruce. It took three minutes and seventeen seconds and was totally worth it. This led to various other videos, such as Biggus Dickus, Killer Rabbit, The Bridge of Death, The Knights Who Say 'Ni', Every Sperm is Sacred, Jim Carrey – How Wealthy People Laugh, Will Ferrell as Tiger Woods, Tiger Woods Smashes Camera on Purpose, Dustin Hoffman Tells a Dirty Story on The Late Show with David Letterman, Marilyn Manson on Letterman, Marilyn Manson Speech on Blame Part 2, Bertrand Russell on Religion (1959), and George Carlin on Religion and God.

I then read approximately 400 of the comments people had made about religion, God, George Carlin and mostly, the other commenters. It was strange to be reading a war in reverse, especially as many of the participants were complete fucking idiots who I wouldn't usually have wasted my time with. Then again, they were exactly the sort of idiots I'd spent my life wasting my time with, so I pondered that for a while, realised several hours had gone by, and that I hadn't found Bruce's phone number. I may not have found the number, but at least I was getting an education.

All this learning was making me hungry. I went to the fridge to get a slice of cheese, or maybe ham, noticed a fridge magnet with a picture of a lawnmower on it stuck to the fridge door right at eye level, called myself a fucking idiot and rang the number.

The phone went brrt brrt, brrt brrt, brrt brrt, brrt…

'Hello' a voice creaked back at me.

'Ah. Bruce is it? Wallace Head.'

'Fuck's sake Wally, fucken Dick Head more like it. What the fuck time is it?'

'Not sure Bruce. Would you like me to hang up so I can look at my phone and see what time it is? I don't mind. I can call you back and let you know in a jiffy.'

'Fuck's sake Wally, it's after midnight ya goose.'

'Oh. Sorry. Umm. I just found your number.'

'Are you dying?'

'No. Why would I be?'

'Doesn't matter. Didn't come back, did she? Are you okay or what? Not, like, suicidal or something?'

'No. Why would I be?'

'Well, you just rang me in the middle of the night. Ring me back in the morning okay?'

'Okay. Goodnight Bruce.'

The phone went beep beep beep beep beep beep beep beep beep beep beep beep beep beep beep beep. Then I went to bed. Well, to lounge really. I didn't use the bed any more. The lounge was better. Big, already dirty, near the very large TV so I had company, and best of all, it didn't have the look and smell of a large bed with soiled sheets and various overused and manky-looking sex toys that your wife and her little friends had abandoned there just to piss you off and upset you.

10

Mate, Don't Look Down the Nice Lady's Top

I WOKE UP BORED. It was eleven o'clock. Okay, it was 11.45. I drank a cup of coffee, ate some cheese, drank a cup of coffee, ate some ham, and drank a cup of coffee.

I remembered I was supposed to call Bruce, but remembered he was probably pissed off with me for waking him in the middle of the night, so thought I'd better not. I sat around wishing something would happen. Something didn't.

I considered calling the police. Even a bit of police brutality might be better than being this bored, but my scab had almost finished peeling off, and I decided to wait until it was completely healed. Besides, $150 for Thai food was a bit expensive just to have someone to belittle and then get beaten up by.

The doorbell went ding dong ding dong ... ding dong ding dong ... ding dong ding dong ... ding dong ding dong. I'd never realised it dinged and donged for quite so long before. Before now it had only ever seemed to ding. Or maybe dong. Or perhaps ding dong. At the most ding dong ding dong. I suppose I hadn't paid enough attention.

I thought maybe I should call out 'Just a minute', then quickly change out of my pyjamas into my clothes, but realised I'd slept in my clothes.

I called out, 'Just a minute,' and opened the door.

'Waddaya mean just a minute ya prize dick? You've already opened the door,' said Bruce. 'Well don't just stand there like a fish with its mouth open, go put the jug on mate.'

He may have been right. My timing may have been a little off when it came to door opening, or speaking, or both, as I'd had little practice at either just lately. As I was thinking about this Bruce strode past me, shaking his head, and went to the kitchen to make us some coffee.

I noticed the letterbox was overflowing, and thought awhile about whether I should go and see what was in it. Maybe Masey had written me a letter. Unlikely. A postcard? With a picture of a tongue and a bald rat maybe. Greetings from Lake Tonguebath. Wish you were here at Arselick-By-The-Sea. The Dicks are Getting Bigger at BDSM Resort. I decided against venturing to the letterbox and went to the kitchen instead.

'Would you like a coffee?' I asked Bruce as he handed me a cup of coffee.

'No thanks,' he said. 'Just this one'll do.'

'Perhaps some lunch?' I asked as politely as I could manage.

'It's three o'clock mate,' he said, taking a wide path around some cheese and ham that was still on the floor. 'Been eating at least I see.'

'Oh yes. No shortage of food. Would you like some cheese? Or some ham perhaps? There's an egg too, I think, but I'm not really sure how to cook it.'

He slowly shook his head and he fastly rolled his eyes and he said, 'Ahhh Wally. Jeez. Lounge room mate. Second thoughts, outside. It fucken stinks in here. Ever thought of opening a window?'

We went out to the back yard and sat under the pergola near the little fountain of Michelangelo's David peeing on the Buddha's belly.

I should have realised Masey was going kinky back then.

We were drinking our coffee and wondering what to say. Well, I was wondering what to say. Bruce may just have been drinking his coffee and not saying anything. I don't really know. I'm not him.

He finished his coffee. 'Righto,' he said. 'Let's get you sorted. Heard from your missus?'

'Not exactly. I mean, I, umm, no.'

'Right. Well, she's gone then, and you're all upset and dunno what to do and you've let your life go to shit. Been going to work?'

'Well, I was going to maybe go, umm, tomorrow or,

I ... I mean, I was going to call them and, well, let them know I might, umm...'

'Right. So you've maybe lost your job too. How you off for money? Didn't empty your accounts did she? Mine fucken did.'

'Oh no. I went to the bank yesterday for some cash, and they're sending me new credit cards. Masey must have needed all the old ones. But there's plenty of money in the bank.' I felt quite clever.

'Right. Shit Wally, you got no idea, do ya mate? Can she access all the accounts?'

'Umm, maybe. Oh. No, no she can't, as a matter of fact. She has an account of her own, and I have an account of my own, and we have a joint account.'

'Right. Well if there's anything left in the joint account, you need to take half of it out and put it in your own account, okay? That way you've done nothing wrong, and you haven't been a complete fucking idiot and thrown it all away. Get your keys, we're off to the bank.'

We went to the bank and did some stuff. It was boring, and when I said hello to the girl at the help desk who'd helped me yesterday she pretended not to recognise me, and gave me that look girls give you when they think you're looking down their top, but you're actually not, it's just that you were lost in thought, and... Doesn't matter. At least she didn't slap me.

So we sorted out the accounts, and Masey hadn't taken all the money out, but we did find out that she'd bought a plane ticket to Thailand, which I know isn't Bali, but at least she was kind of truthful because she did say she was going overseas, plus the fact she didn't take all the money out of the account made me feel like I loved and missed her, well a bit, and while I was thinking about it the girl from the bank said 'Unbelievable' and gave me that look again, only worse, before walking away from us, and Bruce said 'Mate, don't look down the nice lady's top. What you need is a few girlfriends. We'll get you sorted tonight.'

So after the boring bank we went to the boring old supermarket and bought some pretty interesting new food, including bread, even though I insisted I had plenty of ham and cheese to last a few days, then we went home.

Bruce told me I might as well learn to cook a bit, and showed me how to cook steak and mashed potato and peas, then we cleaned up the house a bit while he told me all about how hunting for women is done in the twenty-first century, and then we hit the computer.

11
Old Dog, New Tricks

OF COURSE I'd heard of internet dating. Who hasn't? I just didn't know millions of people actually did it. You hear the stories of course, see them on the current affairs shows when Masey tells you to shut up and watch. Aesthetically challenged women who've been fleeced out of their life savings, mortgaged their homes, given all the money to some supposedly European pretty-boy who turns out to really be from Wollongong or Mount Druitt or Bacchus Marsh, and has done the same thing to sixteen other perfectly nice yet also aesthetically challenged lovely ladies who were simply searching for love.

But this was ridiculous.

Page after page of beautiful and, well, possibly beautiful on the inside, women, all looking for love or casual dating or friendship or...

'Or half of every fucking thing you own,' said Bruce. 'The trick is Wally, it's like a buffet meal. Now you don't want it weighing you down, or making you fat ... fatter,' he corrected himself, looking at my slightly paunchy midsection.

'I'm not fat,' I told him. 'I just ... well I'm not ... that fat.'

'You're fine mate, I was just kiddin,' he told me. 'Don't worry. There ain't much competition really, not at our age. You've got hair, a flash car, money coming out your arse and you're tall. Be a bastard to be short. Easier for tall blokes. You'll be fine. Now, what sorta sheilas do you fancy?'

'Umm. Masey?'

'You idiot. She's not on here, is she? Then again, maybe she is. But she hates you, remember? So. Who else?'

I pointed to a brunette with a happy smile. 'Well, that one there looks quite good. How about her?'

Bruce clicked on the profile, pointed at the words FINANCIALLY SECURE AND SEEKING SAME, and said, 'No fucken way mate. Gold-digger. Lesson one. In internet dating profile language, "financially secure" translates to Already fucked over at least one poor bastard, and "seeking same" means Looking for her next target. Who else?'

'That one,' I said, pointing to a brunette with a happy smile.

'It's the same one, ya fucken dickhead. Point to a different one.'

'Can't you choose? There's too much choice Bruce, and you're the one who knows what you're doing. I just want Masey back.'

'And why did she leave mate? Tell me. Why?'

'Well … I don't know … she went all strange lately. Plastic surgery, and reading these stupid erotic books and trying to get me to dress up, then even inviting her weird friends around that night for some sort of sex party. I don't know, I guess she was … bored?'

'Exactly. So if she's bored of you, and you really want her back, how do you do something about it Wal?'

'Umm … ah … well, maybe … fuck, I don't know. Read the stupid books and dress up in the stupid outfits?'

'Too late mate, she's already gone. You gotta do what she's doing, only bigger and better. You gotta become the star of the internet dating world, the ride-em-cowboy of the rope and handcuffs mummy-porn set. You gotta become Wally Head, King of the Bed.'

'And how do I do that?'

'Practice, Wally-me-lad. Practice. Like it or not mate, those books she's been reading are all they talk about right now. You want the women, you read the books. Most blokes are too fucken stupid to do it, they reckon it's beneath em or something. But the smart bloke finds out what the women want, and gives it to em, right? Just the first book'll do, they're fucken awful. Rather tighten your dick in a vice than read all three. Then again, that might even be in one of em actually.'

I looked at the screen, looked at Bruce, got lost in thoughts of ropes and red shoes and leather underpants and whether it could all be worth it, and when I remembered to look back at the real world Bruce was looking at me as if I'd been trying to look down his top, but at least he didn't slap me, and I just said, 'Okay,' and that was that. I became Grasshopper to Bruce's Master Po. Except that Bruce wasn't blind, and I didn't call him Old Man, and he didn't call me Grasshopper, and he didn't have a pebble I had to snatch, and the only snatch involved was ... okay ... really I was more like an old dog, and he was like The Dog Whisperer, and I was about to learn some new tricks.

Woof!

12

It Makes Her Orgasm You Know

IF I WAS an old dog learning new tricks, I must have been a greyhound, because Bruce trained me like an athlete. He gave me two days to read the book, as well as making me go for long walks while he talked seduction tactics. He attempted to teach me to cook, and made me do all sorts of casual, normal, natural-looking yet interesting stuff while he took photos to put on my dating profile. Like sit on his motorbike and look natural. Sit in my Lexus and look natural. Stir the stir-fry and look natural, even though I'd accidentally just put my thumb and index finger on the edge of the wok and the strongest smell in the kitchen was now coming from what used to be my skin and flesh.

But reading the book was the most difficult thing I ever had to do. Yes, I know, what an easy life I must have had if the hardest thing I ever did was read a book—but until you've read the thing, you have no idea of the sheer literary torture that it inflicts upon its readers.

It makes The Cat Sat on the Mat look like War and Peace, or Anna Karenina, or Bleak House, or ... well, it sucks. And not in the good way. It fucking sucks. I'm not really getting it across am I? It's like falling into a gigantic pile of poo, done by a herd of elephants who've been force fed laxatives and tranquillisers and poo, really stinky poo, and being told the only way to save yourself is to keep swimming through this liquid shit mess, and just drink your way through till it's gone. All of it. Hardest thing I ever did. But I did it. All of it. But only Book One.

Just give me a minute will you? I'm traumatised.

It's not the sex. The sex in that book wasn't of interest, beyond the type of interest one would have if they saw, let's say, a tree trying to fuck a sheep. I mean, it was just silly. The sex itself mostly consisted of the guy does this or that or whatever, it never mattered what, because anything he did resulted in the girl having an orgasm. Not just any orgasm, mind you, but body-shatteringly intense, delicious, turbulent, agonising, exhausting, violent, all-consuming orgasms. Well, they probably are the best kind. She has them when he fucks her. When he says her name. When he touches her shoulder. Or her face. When she notices his lips quirk up, purse up, or pucker up. When he tweaks her nipples. When he whips her tight little peach of an arse. And he keeps hitting her, which for some reason makes her have orgasms too. He stalks her, she orgasms. He belittles her, same again. He offers to hit her, or not hit her, or thinks about hitting her, or tells her he knows he's a bastard for hitting her, more orgasms. She even has them when he whispers, mutters or murmurs. And he does SO FUCKING MUCH whispering, muttering and murmuring. No wonder either. It makes her orgasm you know.

Now I'm really very sorry, but my sexual knowledge and experience have been somewhat limited. Maybe I'm not that normal, maybe Masey isn't. Considering my own experience of assisting, aiding and abetting a female in search of such turbulent and agonising orgasms, the immortal words of the greatest philosopher ever known are brought to mind. Was it not the wise Billy Connolly who, when educating us on trying to locate the G-spot, announced that ye could nay fucken find it wearing a wetsuit and a diver's helmet?

Yet here's this young girl, well she's orgasming here, and orgasming there, at parties and in cars and in churches and helicopters and zoos and anywhere fucking else she goes that he happens to be anywhere near her? Or think about her? Or she about him? Or…?

Sorry. I'm traumatised. But that's not even why. Why? You want to know why? You really want to know why the greatest insult ever inflicted on literature traumatised me? I can't even tell you. Too horrible. Read it yourself and you'll know. I take it back. Don't read it. Seriously, it's not worth it. But fuck you if you still want to know, and are stupid enough to read it, fuck you. Read it then, see if I care. I tried to stop you.

But I warn you now, actually, not yet, this deserves a whole fucking chapter of its own. I can give you only one worthwhile piece of advice — ignore it at your peril. Do NOT read it, because it will introduce a concept to your life that you, just like me, had never previously considered.

Fucking brace yourself.

13
Un-Un-Un-Un-Un-Un-Un-Un-Un-Un-Un-Un-Un-Un-Un

No matter how much you want to, you can never unread a book.

14
He Made Me!

SORRY. Should never have mentioned the 'book.'

But seriously, if you'd ever read the stinkiest, most horrible pile of...

Okay. Breathe. I survived. Here I am, survived to tell the story. Telling the story. Not the fucking story in the fucking stupid fucking stupid 'book' that Master Bruce Fucking Po the Fucking Dog-Whispering Fucking Bastard Shitface Dog-Fucking Lawn-Mowing...

Sorry. I'll get over it. Bruce is my friend. He helped me a lot. But he made me read that fucking pile of fucking vomitus and...

Sorry.

Sorry. Breathe Wallace. Breathe.

Right.

I'll be fine.

Let's continue this tomorrow shall we?

15
Adjusting Yourself

CHAPTER 15 has been left intentionally blank while Wallace has treatment to allow him to readjust to society post Modern Literary Sensation.

16
Longer Than We Thought

DITTO. Treatment taking longer than we thought.

17

Our Collective Willies

Hi, I'm Wally, and I just love puppies and pussies and purple ropes. There's nothing quite like relaxing after a long — yes ladies, I said long — day in bed, with a nice kiss and cuddle of some puppies, and a playful pounce on a particularly pretty pussy. And the purple rope? Well, I promise not to tie it too tight.

WELL YES. That's what my dating site profile said. I know. It seemed a bit much at the time too. But as Bruce explained, if I wanted Masey back, I had to act fast.

Now, I would not have thought that sort of thing would bring anything to a man but another visit from our rather tiny yet more than a little vicious local constabulary.

I was wrong.

I can tell you, there is certainly no shortage of beautiful, and … umm … yes … beautiful on the inside, women, who are more than willing to play ropesies and blindfolds with an average looking, reasonably well off, hopefully well-endowed male who's game enough to risk a second helping of police brutality, a stern reprimand from his mother (who it turns out was on the same dating site), and repeated funny looks and sideways glances in local shopping centres and cafés, just because he was upfront about what he wanted. Not that it was what I truly wanted. It was what I pretended I wanted, and what Bruce cajoled me into saying I wanted, but to me it was simply a means to an end, an end where I'd get what I really wanted, which was Masey back home, and everything back to normal. Ish. Normal-Ish.

I mean, I wasn't so sure I even wanted my job any more, and while I wanted Masey back, I knew I didn't want her to treat me like a moron the way she has the past few years, and I certainly didn't want her to be as unhappy as she had been for as long as I could remember. Actually, I wasn't quite sure what I wanted back, but as Bruce said, it was no time to be dwelling on the past. I was about to fuck my way to a brilliant new future. To go where no National Supply Manager of one of the biggest food supply chains in the world has gone before. To become a shining example to other not terribly good-looking and somewhat downtrodden men of what can be achieved when we chuck in our jobs, tell lies about what we want on the internet, take our collective willies in one hand

and a length of purple rope in the other, and say I AM MAN. And all I want is to give you a jolly good rogering. And maybe a few rope burns.

As a fifty-one year old man who'd only ever slept with one woman, that was going to be an experience. If only I'd have known how much of an experience…

I'd have bought larger condoms.

18
The Shape of a Heart

DESPITE IT being my dating profile, my computer, my house, and my life, Bruce wouldn't actually allow me to have any say in what was going on.

'Fuck you Wally mate,' he said. 'If you won't even choose your own women you're not driving the computer. That's only for us big boys.'

I was nervous of course. I'd only ever dated two other women before Masey. One of them had hit me, the other one had tried to get her brother to hit me. I never did find out why. Masey said I'd probably made them feel unattractive by not making a move on them. Well, why would I have made a move on them? I'd only been out with each of them twice. Surely a goodnight kiss would have been impertinent and far too forward.

And so, due to my limited experience, and my supposed lack of 'knowing what the fuck' I was doing, Bruce decided I needed a practice run, with someone around to help when I got into trouble, and arranged for us to go on a double date. He was chatting to a 'scrubber' online for himself, and she happened to mention she had a friend who'd just joined up. Photos were sent here and there, and before I knew it I had Bruce telling me what to wear—which was even worse than having Masey ordering me around, as he actually checked that I'd put the leather underpants on before we left for the pub.

Distrustful fucker.

Also, he'd made me do an oral test about what I'd learned from reading that thing I'm not going to mention.

Bastard. I'll give him fucking dog-whisperer. I … It's okay. I'm fine. Just fine. Really.

So there I was, in my shiny suit, my fat tie, my leather fucking underpants and shiny pointy shoes with big silver buckles. Bruce was driving the Lexus, because I was too nervous to do anything but run to the dunny every five minutes for another nervous whatever, and it now seemed unavoidable—no matter what I did, going on a date with a woman who wasn't Masey was really going to happen.

The car park was packed, so he parked the Lexus in one of the disabled parking spots right near the main entrance to the pub, and I said, 'You can't park here, we're not disabled.'

'That's fucken debatable Wally,' he said, 'and besides, those disabled fuckers are always parking in our spots.'

We walked inside. I set my face to look relaxed yet intelligent, so I wouldn't look like I was shitting myself. I hoped no-one could tell.

Bruce looked at me and said, 'Wally ya dumb fuck, stop trying to look like you're trying not to shit your trousers. Just relax mate, we probably won't even like this pair of scrubbers. They always look older than their photos, we'll just have one drink with them and leave.'

And so, anxiety temporarily gone, we strode in together, two confident men in search of a drink, a hello, a goodbye, and the slight chance of sex with some scrubbers.

We walked in. It was busy. Noisy. Dark. And everything happening much too quickly. Bruce was on the phone. Bruce was off the phone.

'Back corner,' he yelled over the music.

I followed him to the back corner. Both women were there. They actually looked pretty good. Bruce's one had big pretend boobies, spilling all out of her dress, and was called Rosemary. Bruce sat down beside her, and his eyes tried to push me around to the other side of the table, to sit next to my one.

I stood very still. No fight, but plenty of flight. No wonder the Tiny Policeman had hit me with his truncheon. Probably needed to stop me from running away. I wished he were here now. I wondered just where he was, who he was hitting, wondered what it must be like to be five foot four and carry a large truncheon, and…

'Wally! I said sit down mate. This is Therese and Rosemary. Try not to scare them away while I go get us all a drink. His brain stops working in noisy places, but he's a good fella, really Therese. Back in a minute ladies.' His eyes threatened me with my imminent death. Obviously I was not allowed to scare the nice ladies away while he was gone.

'Hello Theresa,' I said.

'It's Therese,' she said, turning away to look at … a blank wall. I looked at it too, wondering if I was supposed to use the striking blankness of the wall to spark up a witty conversation. Then I wondered if that might scare the women away, so I didn't say anything, and looked at Therese instead. She was extremely attractive. Possibly forty-five, thick dark hair, light olive skin and a tall, slender figure without a hint of plastic surgery in sight.

'So,' said Rosemary, giggling. 'Purple ropes, Wallace?'

'I … umm … well, yes Rosemary, I've always liked the colour purple, ever since, umm…' It was quite coincidental I suppose, because I could feel my face going a fairly dark shade of purple as I struggled for something to say, and I just kind of ground to a halt, and looked at Therese, who was looking at me as if I'd been looking down her top. She shook her rather attractive head, and somewhere in the middle of wondering what shade of reddish purple I must be, and how Rosemary seemed rather too much like Masey in that pretentious plastic-boobed facelifted way, and wishing Bruce would hurry back so we could drink our drinks and leave, Therese's lovely thick hair came away from her eyes.

Away. From her eyes.

Her eyes.

I fell right into them, completely lost in their thick creamy deep luscious brown, and I thought of one of those fancy coffees they make in cafés, where the top is all frothy and gorgeous, and in it's the shape of a heart, or a leaf, or an old sailing ship, or any number of things I couldn't think of at the time, because I was noticing — as I fell back out of the eyes, what with them rolling violently in disgust at me and all, and the head they were in turning quickly back to the blank wall — there were wrinkles around the eyes. Lovely beautiful honest wrinkles.

And I was quite suddenly glad to be there.

'You have tiny wrinkles near your eyes,' I said.

'You have a tiny brain near your arse,' she said.

That was when Bruce came back with the drinks, and I should've been immensely relieved that I hadn't done anything to upset the women and make them leave, but I didn't even think about that. I was too busy being slightly in love.

19
Trying Not To Watch

The night was going well. Bruce and Rosemary seemed to be hitting it off rather nicely. For a while I thought maybe they weren't. Sometimes it's hard to tell. We drank our first drinks. Beer all round. Bruce and Rosemary laughed and chatted. Therese obviously liked me. I could tell by the way she completely ignored me. I offered to go to the bar for a second round of drinks. Beer for Bruce and Rosemary. And Therese — Therese — said she'd have water.

'Great minds think alike,' I said.

'I'll have orange juice,' Therese said.

'Me too,' I said.

'Good,' she said. 'I'll have water.'

I got us both water.

By now Bruce and Rosemary were ignoring us completely. Because they were kind of supposed to be getting to know each other, this was perfectly natural. They didn't really seem to like each other though.

I could tell Therese liked me a lot. I hadn't been this well ignored by a woman I'd just met since I was first introduced to Masey on a mutual friend's yacht all those years ago. This was going great. I played it really cool and ignored her right back. Yeah. While the cat's away the ... I mean, the early bird gets the ... I mean...

Rosemary said, 'I'm going to the bar.'

Bruce said, 'Are you fucken kidding? I'm not even half finished my second drink.'

Rosemary said, 'Not my fault you're a softcock nancy-boy Brucie. You'd better drink faster. I'll get us all a beer.'

'Not for me,' said Therese.

'Not for her,' said me.

'What's it got to do with you?' said Therese.

'I meant ... umm ... what?'

'I'll have a beer then,' said Therese, giving me a filthy look. This was going better than I expected.

'Great minds think alike,' I said, but nobody was listening, because Rosemary had left for the bar, Therese had rolled her eyes at me and gone with her, Bruce had walked off to the dunny, and I was the only one there. Also, it had taken me a while to think of anything to say.

Rosemary came back with a beer for everybody, plus a Wild Turkey chaser for herself.

She skulled the beer, then downed the chaser in one gulp. Bruce called her a drunk and a lush. She called Bruce a softcock again, and told him he shouldn't be letting a little girl outdrink him. He told her she was a loudmouth bitch, and that it was lucky he knew a way of shutting her up, which he'd be only too pleased to demonstrate later. She told him he had tickets on himself. He told her he used to have tickets on himself, but they'd sold out in the first hour.

I tried to ignore them as their bickering was becoming unpleasant, but I didn't want to leave. The ignoring between Therese and I was going wonderfully. I decided it was time to gradually make my move, and planned to get her attention by the performance of a highly planned series of actions, the first of which was moving my beer, which was still almost full, closer to hers, so I could accidentally brush her lovely lean fingers when she reached for her drink. It went well. Nobody noticed me move my glass. Should have been a private detective. Maybe a spy.

Rosemary and Bruce were getting busy, caning each other with lots of nasty insults. By now they'd progressed to calling each other Fucktard and Stinkpuss. I saw Therese reaching for her drink, and ever so nonchalantly reached for mine at the same time, unfortunately overreaching slightly and knocking both glasses to the floor.

'Taxi!' called Bruce, Rosemary and several other people around us.

'You stupid idiot,' said Therese.

'Sorry about that,' I said, trying to use my fat grey tie to wipe up what I'd spilled on Therese's lap, which was difficult because I had to bend forward so the tie would reach her lap, and I accidentally had my face extremely close to her lovely and obviously very real breasts.

'Get the fuck away from me you moron,' said Therese. 'Oh, why did I agree to this?'

'I don't know,' I said. 'I'm not you.'

Bruce and Rosemary were completely ignoring me, totally engrossed as they were in some very nasty name-calling. Therese had stormed off to the bathroom, so it seemed like a good time to duck under the table to pick up the pieces of glass.

I ducked under the table.

That's interesting, I thought.

That's interesting, I didn't say. Mostly because it renders a man somewhat speechless when he probably shouldn't be looking, and wishes he weren't looking, and can't believe what he's seeing, because the thing he's seeing is his friend and mentor's master of ceremonies standing proudly, staring out at him from above the woman's hand that's sliding up and down the length of it.

Well, what would you have done? I could still hear their voices. Above the slapping sound.

Obviously I couldn't come out, they'd know I'd seen them. I stayed, trying not to watch the cock-and-hand train wreck. Trying not to watch. Trying not to watch. Trying not to watch.

'Ya fucken softcock.'

Trying not to watch.

'Ya filthy moll'

Trying not to watch.

'Ya stinken monkey-fucker.'

Trying not to watch.

'Ya ... ya ... yayayaaaaaaa whoa baybeeee, faaaaaarrrrrk,' went Bruce as his fine upstanding citizen exploded under the table. Well, not completely exploded. I mean, that would have been even more horrible. Yuck. Imagine that.

And what about the news!

> 'This is the news. Earlier this evening a one-eyed trouser-snake ... ah, my apologies ... I should have said penis. Earlier this evening an erect penis exploded under a table in a rather stinky pub in a leafy suburb a short distance from the city. Names have not been released, possibly to protect the guilty. The only eye witness ... that is to say, the only eye witness that didn't explode is Wallace Head, a recently unemployed man with very few prospects who was out on his first date since his wife had left him. Interviewed after the event, Mister Head stated, "It was the scariest and most horrible thing I've seen

since a recent run-in with a rather vicious yet remarkably cute bald rat."

'And what exactly were you up to under the table Mister Head? There is some speculation that you're a filthy pervert who, working in partnership with your friend and mentor Mister Bruce "Master Po" Lawnmower Man, were conspiring by fair means or foul to get off by watching him, umm, get off under the table.'

'I didn't. I mean, I wasn't. I mean, I'd just been trying to mop up a drink I'd spilled on the beautiful woman who was ignoring me, and…'

'What the fuck are you doing crawling around under the table?' asked Therese, 'And where has Rosemary gone?'

'Umm. I … was … umm … I wasn't here when they left,' I said, which was technically partly true, as I wasn't completely there, as I was, in some way, possibly on some other plane of existence, being interviewed for the news.

'Great,' she said. 'Now how the fuck do I get home?'

I was going to say, 'I don't know, I'm not you,' but I didn't, because she'd already turned her back on me and taken her phone out and was trying to make a call.

I could only hope she wasn't calling a news crew.

20
The Train Wreck

SHE LOOKED SO PRETTY, just something about the way she was standing there ignoring me, it made me think of Masey when I first knew her, and I knew right then Therese was the girl for me. For now of course. Just temporary, like. Until Masey came back, which of course she soon would, because...

'They're out in the car-park,' she said.

'Who?' I said.

She didn't answer, and technically I didn't see this, because she'd already started to leave and was three steps in front of me, but she rolled her eyes. I really loved the way she rolled her eyes. Whether I saw it or not. I would have told her, but by then she was halfway across the room, and I'd have had to yell really loudly, and some drunk person may have taken offence and decided to fight me. And I really don't like fighting people. Mostly because me fighting people has only ever consisted of people hitting me, then me falling down. Although a couple of times, for variety I suppose, the people who were hitting me then added kicking me to their repertoire. So that's why I don't like fighting people. Therese was all the way across the room now, and I realised I should follow her. I followed her.

I caught up a little way into the car-park. Near my car actually. They were all near it. Well, technically, one of them was on it, or at least her rear end was—and the shortness of her skirt, and something about the way Bruce was pushing various parts of himself up against her made me really hope she was wearing underwear. I wanted to say something like, "Excuse me Rosemary, but not knowing where your behind has been or anything, I'm a little uncomfortable with it being all over the paintwork of my car"—but quickly weighing up the possibility of her saying, "Sorry Wallace" against the possibility of her becoming one of those people who want to fight me, I decided against it.

'Let's go Wally, you're driving mate,' said Bruce.

'Driving where?' said Therese.

'Driving where?' said me, but nobody listened, because Bruce was talking louder than I was, and at the same time—and apart from at work, nobody ever much seems to listen to me anyway.

'Home James,' said Bruce. 'Your home.'

I would have pointed out to him that my name isn't James, but I didn't get a chance to speak because Therese was speaking, and I was admiring the way the wrinkles near her eyes and mouth moved as she spoke.

I have no idea what she said, mesmerised as I was, or maybe it was the two beers, or perhaps Bruce had slipped something into my beer to make me more fun, or...

'Well come on, let's go,' two different people were saying almost at the same time, although I didn't really care because neither of them were Therese, and I was really quite engrossed in the way she was rolling her eyes.

So then I was driving. It was great. Therese sat in the front with me, because Bruce and Rosemary were in the back. I was pretending Therese was my girlfriend, and we were on our way to the beach for a romantic moonlit stroll, after which we'd either make love under the stars, or if we didn't want to get sand in our bits, decide instead to hold back our animal passions until returning to my place, where we'd lie naked together in front of an open fire, making love on a bearskin rug, or ... that was when I accidentally looked in the rear view mirror, and saw what Bruce and Rosemary were doing. It looked like we might soon be on our way to another train wreck.

'So Therese,' I said, tearing my eyes away from the train wreck. 'How have you enjoyed your evening so far?'

She rolled her eyes, shook her head, and turned on the radio.

'Would you like to choose something from my music collection?' I asked. I'm not sure she heard me. There was a lot of slurping coming from the back seat.

She turned up the radio.

We drove the rest of the way to my place in silence, if you can class silence as a very loud radio and the occasional slurping noise.

I parked in the driveway. We went inside. Bruce offered to give Rosemary a tour of the house. They went upstairs and didn't come back.

Therese looked at the art.

'This is horrible,' she said, shaking her head.

'I know,' I said, nodding mine.

'Your wife's?'

'Yes.'

'Horrible.'

'Would you like a cup of tea?'

'Best suggestion I've heard all night,' she said. Maybe she even smiled.

When I came back with the tea, Therese had some classical music playing on the stereo, and was relaxing in a recliner with her shoes off. I put the tea beside her, and this time, she really did smile.

'So,' she said. 'When did your wife leave?'

And that was it. I started to cry.

21
All I Can Give

I DON'T KNOW WHY it happened. I knew it was unmanly, and that a woman like Therese—who, after all was only there to meet me because she was under the impression I was a rough, tough, ride-em-cowboy sex fiend with leather underpants and a purple rope—would be so turned off by this display of weakness she'd walk right out the door and never speak to me again. Not to mention the distinct possibility she'd soon be letting the whole internet dating world know what a pretender I was.

I would never have sex again, that was clear now.

Worse, I had fallen into a horrible pit of my own emotions, and they were wet. Wet eyes, wet face, wet shirt, wet person. Wet brain. Soggy. Masey was all I knew. She was never coming back. It had turned out that, without Masey there continually telling everyone, including me, how much I loved my job, that I did not in fact like my job at all. It was a horrible soul-destroying job, where everything was just numbers, including the people. The people! Worse, my son was gone from my home, gone from the country, gone from my life. My dear, dear little boy. Grown up, gone from my life before I managed to find the time to really get to know him.

I was what? I'd become a pretender, a man who told lies online so that strangers might consent to have some sort of weird sex with him, which would for some warped reason make his wife come back to him and be, not the woman she'd become in the past few years, but some ideal person that was possibly never actually her to begin with, just the object a stupid, stupid man had placed on a pedestal to worship.

I cried like a girl, like a baby, like a cat in the night. A cat that strongly objects to the atrocities being inflicted upon it, but knows it can do nothing but cry. But unlike the cat, I knew I deserved this, and that just made me cry more.

At some point, during all this crying, I felt a small warm hand in mine, and looked through the tears and saw that Therese hadn't left. Which made me cry at the futility of it all, and the beauty of strangers who care about others, and I tried really hard to stop crying, but that made me make a really weird snorting sound, which made us both laugh, so now I was crying while I was laughing, and probably had all sorts of horrible gunk on my face that I didn't want to think about but couldn't help it, and I wanted to run to the bathroom to wash my face, but didn't want to let go of Therese's hand, so

I kind of just hid my face in my shirt, which made my neck hurt when I sobbed, or hiccupped, or whatever that weird noise was, then everything kind of went quiet.

Then I heard strange noises and laughter coming from upstairs, and I looked at Therese, and it was more than a little weird. And she said, 'I'll just turn the music up shall I?'

So she got up and attended to that, and I went to the kitchen and washed my face a bit, and came back in and said I was sorry.

And we talked about stuff. We talked about marriage and divorce, and James leaving home, and how it feels to find out you've been living a lie. Turned out she'd been through a bad marriage and divorce herself, and that when it came to living a lie, she wrote the book, but she didn't elaborate any further. And she told me she's not into that whole rope and blindfolds thing at all, that Rosemary's her new neighbour, and she only came along tonight because she felt sorry for her. And that she had no idea what she was getting into until after they arrived at the pub.

So I told her I wasn't into that stuff either, and she said to call her Tess.

We talked for hours, and when she eventually decided she'd call a taxi, I insisted on driving her home, and asked her if maybe she'd like to go out sometime, maybe just see a movie or something, or go for a walk, or maybe not walk, but…

'No,' she said. 'I won't go out with you Wal. Your wife's just left, you need to deal with it. You need to find out who you are, you need to heal. You need to read fifty self-help books then talk about them like you know what life's all about, and then you need to realise none of those books made your life any better. That's the way this thing works. You don't need to be seeing anybody. You need to find out who you are. Tell you what. I'll be your friend. We'll go for a walk once a week, and you'll tell me who you think you are. Once a week for an hour. And I'll go out with men who aren't you, and I'll tell you about them, and maybe ask what you think, and you won't get jealous. Ever. And you'll be a good friend to me, just as I am to you. That's all I can give you. Yes or no?'

'Yes.'

And then I drove Tess home.

22
The Punishment Room

WELL, you know what all that means, don't you? She likes me. A lot. Maybe loves me. A little. Well, early days, but she wants to spend time with me, right? She saw me at my worst — well, maybe not drunk and naked in the bushes being kicked in the k'nackers by a vicious bald rat with red shoes and legs like a horse — but certainly with shit in my head, and tears and snot all over my face, and...

Hmm, maybe she did just want to be friends after all. But I wasn't gonna let that stop me. Tess. What a beautiful name. Tess. Like test, but with a different end. I'll show her a different end — I mean, not like a sexual end, I'm not being dirty or anything, I mean, just a — like a happy ending, a romantic one, where the guy gets the girl, and ... mmm Tess. What a beautiful name. Like testicles, but with, umm, prettier hair and not so itchy and scratchy, or ... mmm Tess. What a beautiful name.

I drove her home, and when we got there she wrote her number on a piece of paper, and as she wrote it I was looking at the soft skin on her lovely long neck, and I said, 'So, umm, any chance of a kiss goodnight?'

Well, her voice went all scary bossy and she said, 'Do you want to be friends or not?'

'Well of course I do,' I said. 'Can't blame a fella for trying can you? How about a friendly hug instead?'

Then, in the sexiest voice I ever heard, she said, 'Oh Wally, you're irresistible. I can't wait to get my hands on you. Let's go inside. I'll put on my catsuit and introduce you to the punishment room!'

'I...I...Really?' I asked.

'No Wally, not really. I was pulling your leg,' and she rolled her eyes and kissed me on the cheek and said, 'Bye friend, call me on Thursday, we'll go for a walk,' and she got out of my car and went into her house.

I watched her walk inside. Sexy walk. Don't you just love that deer-like way a well put-together woman walks at the end of a long night when they're carrying their shoes instead of wearing them? Hot as. Makes you wanna shine some headlights on them. She walked up the stairs, then turned and waved before closing the door, and I was pretending she was my girlfriend, then it occurred to me that I was kind of an idiot for doing all this pretending. After all, I could still feel the sticky glow of her kiss on my cheek, so I decided the reality of that was better than anything pretend. And she sounded like she knew a whole lot more about life than I did, so I'd maybe just do what she said.

I drove home, took off my stupid clothes, including the even stupider than stupid leather underpants, and dreamed about lions while I slept on the lounge.

23
Well It Wasn't About Lions

I HAVE NO IDEA why I dreamed about lions, or why I woke up with what I'd like to think was an enormous hard-on. Well, we all like to think we're a bit above average. Ask anybody.

'How big's yours?'

'Bit above average.'

Everyone you ever ask. So I'm told. I only ever asked two people. One of them said a bit above average, the other one hit me.

It's always a weird time — that bit when you're not asleep and you're not awake either. Some of the time I spent between being asleep and being awake I was trying to stay asleep so I could finish the dream, and some of the time I was hoping no-one was secretly watching me and the hard-on, and some of the time I was hoping the lion and the hard-on weren't related, and feeling guilty that maybe they were, but even though I really didn't want anyone seeing me, I was still too tired to completely wake up, or at least wake up enough to find the sheet and cover myself.

What's the deal with that anyway? The weird dreams thing. And what's so bad about it, seriously? There's worse things, right? Like… Okay, I'm not saying. You really can't say shit without people assuming it's some sort of sick confession you're trying out on them, wondering what they'll say — to tell the truth I'm already a little concerned I mentioned the lions. Forget the lions. Then again, at least a lion is something that's big and tough and can look after itself, and the worst one might get called would be a giant pussy-fucker, or maybe a fucker of giant pussies, or…

'What's a bloke gotta do to get some breakfast round here?' called Bruce from the top of the stairs. 'Struck out with Tracey I see.'

'Her name's Therese,' I said, pulling the sheet up from where it had fallen to the floor, the better to cover myself with.

Too late.

'Holy fucken donkey dick,' said Bruce, pointing in my direction as he descended the stairs. 'What the fuck did you get that thing transplanted off of? Last time I saw something like that was when I went to the horse races.'

'I…I…'

'Just don't point it in my direction Wally. You got a licence for that weapon? Jeez, make a bloke feel totally inadequate why don't you? Fuck mate. Oh well, mine'd still be considered huge in the insect world. No wonder Tracey left. Saw that thing and started running I reckon. Know I fucken would have.'

'I don't suppose you'd like to go to the kitchen and put on some coffee … and stop making jokes about my private parts would you?'

'Reckon I better. Too dangerous in here. A bloke could get choked by a python or something.'

At least the conversation had the effect of shrinking Little Wallace back to a normal state, and I hadn't been questioned about what I'd been thinking or dreaming about in order for him to have gotten into the state he was in. That would not have been good. The last thing I needed early in the morning was to be ridiculed about my dreams. I dressed, drained the old frill-neck lizard, washed my face and went to the kitchen, where Bruce was making one of his signature spattery messes. Bacon, eggs, baked beans, toast and butter magically spread from one end of the kitchen to the other. He was great at making messes, but was yet to clean one up.

Don't mention the lions, don't mention the lions, don't mention the lions, I thought all the way from the bathroom to the kitchen.

He backed against the side of the pantry as I entered the kitchen, reeling away from me in mock horror, then pretended to circle around where a three foot long penis would have protruded in front of me in order to hand me a cup of coffee.

'What were you dreaming about Bigboy? Musta been a fucken beauty.'

'Well it wasn't about lions,' I thought I thought.

'Waddaya mean lions,' he said.

'What?' I asked. Clearly, one of us was confused.

'It wasn't about lions, you just said.'

'What?'

'Yer fucken mad,' he said. 'Don't show Rosemary that cock. You'll never escape alive. Sick puppy that one. What happened to Tracey?'

'Therese,' I said. 'I drove her home at 5am, she wanted to get some sleep.'

'Rogered her half to death with that thing first, did you? Goddamn Wally, why didn't you tell me you were harbouring a dangerous criminal down there? Always the quiet ones ain't it?'

'What? I mean, umm, no! I mean, she … we … we were talking about stuff all night. She's a very nice girl, I'll have you know. We're going for a walk on Thursday. She just wants to be friends. She's a very nice girl. A very nice girl indeed.'

Bruce was just standing there, looking at me with his mouth open. Which was a bit disgusting really, as it was full of half-chewed bacon and eggs and toast, which he'd stopped chewing so he could pretend to be dumbstruck by standing there speechless with his mouth open.

'Okay,' he said, which made little bits of food fly out of his mouth. And a couple of big bits. Then, after chewing a bit and swallowing a lot, 'That's all very lovely Wally-me-lad, but what have we learned mate?'

'Umm. That there are still nice women out there, and that if Masey doesn't come back, a decent person like me might be able to get one to spend some time with him?' I felt quite smart, and looked at him hopefully.

'NO, DICKHEAD. We've learned why your missus wrote softcock in foot-high red letters on your bathroom mirror and left you. We've learned that you haven't been paying attention. Don't make me make you read the second book in that fucken series. Cos I'll do it. Seriously mate, what the fuck were you thinking? You were supposed to shag the woman within an inch of her life. Which, I might add, would have been a very real prospect given the fact that huge fat cock of yours belongs on a donkey.'

'But...'

'No fucken buts, mate. Actually, yes fucking butts. HER butt. And the next woman's butt. I've a good mind to march you upstairs now and let Rosemary have you, only I know you'd never survive it. Woman's a fucken animal. Didn't even care where all those sex toys on your bed had been. Thanks for those, by the way. Your missus use em when she wanted something a bit smaller than you did she?'

'I … I … They weren't mine! They belong to the people Masey went away with. Oh Bruce, maybe I'm not cut out for all of this. Maybe I'm just a normal conventional guy who works in a job he hates and comes home and sleeps next to a woman he loves, and has normal conventional sex once every few weeks until he's too old to do it anymore. Maybe…'

'Did somebody mention sex?' asked Rosemary, who had sneaked up on us wearing one of Masey's rather see-through *baby-doll negligees*.

'Good God,' I thought I thought. 'Those look like the exact same *perfectly pert yet pendulously bulbous* breasts as Masey's.'

'Beauties, ain't they,' said Rosemary, drawing herself more upright and proudly thrusting her chest in my direction. 'Went to Doc Hung too did she? He does great work, don't you think?'

'A true craftsman,' said Bruce, licking his lips as his eyes darted from the breasts in question to the framed portrait of Masey on the opposite wall and back again.

I realised I hadn't had enough sleep, was possibly saying what I was thinking I was thinking, rather than thinking what I was thinking then saying what I was thinking I should say—also I may have had a persisting picture of a very scrawny yet extremely vicious lion in my feeble mind—and so I took advantage of a lull in the conversation and escaped to the shower, locking the door behind me just in case these perverted people got it into their heads to follow me.

24
Pulling Yourselves Together

PULL YOURSELF together, I thought, or possibly only thought I thought, as I tried to enjoy the feeling of warm water streaming over me.

Not, pull yourself together now … and a-One, and a-Two, and a One-Two-Three-Four, I thought, or possibly only thought I thought, but really…

This was getting me nowhere. I was confused, and tired, and possibly tired of being confused.

Bruce had been a really good friend to me, had helped to drag me up out of the rut I'd fallen into when Masey left, and I was grateful. He didn't have to help me, but he did so anyway. He was a true friend, and I was lucky to have him. On the other hand he had just defiled my marital bed with an extremely noisy woman with *perfectly pert yet pendulously bulbous* breasts, breasts I didn't want to think about, breasts exactly the same model as Masey's, which maybe meant something in the big scheme of things, and which I should be taking as some sort of sign, but which I couldn't yet think properly about because I hadn't at this point read any of the fifty self-help books

Tess had suggested I would—or was it should?—be reading.

All this thinking about sex was getting too much for me. I wanted to stop thinking about it. Clearly, the best way to stop thinking about sex, I thought, is to have sex. Such are the urges of man. I thought maybe I'd better just rub one out so I'd stop thinking about it. I thought I'd think about Tess while I did. Problem was, I could hear noisy gross Rosemary cackling from the kitchen, and the thought of Rosemary pointing Masey's exact breasts at Bruce through Masey's negligee in Masey's kitchen was making it difficult to concentrate. I gave up and decided that things were going to change around here, but I couldn't really work out which things. Maybe I needed to lay down the law. My house, my rules. I imagined myself marching out of the shower and into the kitchen. Right, I'd say. You, Rosemary. Get out of that *baby-doll negligee*. Okay, she'd say. I thought you'd never ask. Alright then Wally, Bruce would say, that explains why you have no clothes on, but shouldn't you have dried off first?

Maybe I hadn't thought it through.

I took my time showering, thought maybe I'd shave off my beard.

No, I thought back, I'm still quite liking it, and decided to leave it.

Maybe a goatee, I thought.

Maybe tomorrow, I thought back. I realised there were too many of me thinking, and not enough of me doing.

I decided I needed some sleep.

I concurred.

It didn't matter how many of me decided I needed to sleep, what mattered was that I get some. Some sleep I mean. It was a problem. I still couldn't go into my bedroom. My clothes were in the other bedroom, but the bed in there had belonged to James when he was a kid, and was one of those bunk beds, double on the bottom, single on top. It just didn't seem like I could sleep in there either. I'm a big boy now. And none of the other rooms had beds in them. Masey's sewing room. Masey's music room. Masey's dressing room. I'd been sleeping on the lounge since Masey left, but it was no good when people were over.

What about the cabana? I asked.

Well, I suppose I could sleep there, I answered.

It has a comfortable lounge, and a shower and toilet too, I offered as helpfully as I could.

Yes, I'm fully aware of that, thank you, I countered, as appreciatively as I could without being too condescending.

It's settled then, I decided.

Okay, I agreed. I'll sleep in the cabana.

'I'm going to bed,' I called to nobody in particular. On further investigation I'd called it to nobody at all, as it turned out Bruce and Rosemary had left in Bruce's ute while I was showering.

I went to the cabana and slept for a really long time.

25
A Notch on the Bedpost

IT WAS really dark, and my phone was going Ringg Ringg … Ringg Ringg … Ringg Ringg … Ringg Ringg …

'Hello,' I said. I always say that. It's just what I say.

'What are you up to Secretariat?' said a loud voice that seemed familiar, but probably wasn't because they had the wrong number.

'Sorry,' I said. 'Nobody here by that name.'

'Very fucken funny Wally ya goose. Now stop fucken around, what are you doing?' asked Bruce. I could tell it was him. Nobody else in the world swears that much when they're not even angry.

'Well I'm not sure,' I answered. 'It's dark. I don't know where I am.'

'Well you better fucken find out mate,' he told me. 'We got another double date tonight. You get the chance to redeem yourself after last night's piss-poor showing. Have a tub and I'll see you in half an hour.'

'But … what? Who? You didn't…'

'You're in luck Wally. Rosemary's got another friend for you, the one that was supposed to come last night but couldn't. Sure thing this one. Even you can't fuck it up she reckons.'

'But I…'

'No buts Wally. Time to use what you've learned. Now be a good boy and go get ready.'

The phone went beep beep beep beep beep beep beep beep beep beep beep beep beep beep beep.

I hate when that happens. My eyes had adjusted to the dark and I realised I was in the cabana. Maybe I could live here. It was like a little cubby house, except big. I had a cubby house once, when I was ten. Or nine, I can't remember. Or maybe…

I had to get ready. I had a date. But what about Tess? I liked Tess. But she wasn't my girlfriend, and she even said she wouldn't be my girlfriend. And I wanted Masey back. Bruce was right. I went inside the house, had a quick shower and dressed. Why not? Masey had left me. Tess didn't want me. I was a free agent. I had a big tonsil-tickler. Slightly above average, I hoped. Bruce was a real joker. Also, he was enthusiastic, and had a way of making you feel good about yourself, even when he called you a dickhead. No wonder women liked him. And he was probably right. It was the only way to get Masey back. For the third time, I dressed in the shiny suit and the fat grey tie. But not the leather underpants. I couldn't find them. Probably because I didn't look in the laundry basket. At the bottom. Wrapped in a towel. Not that I'd know, because I didn't look there.

I didn't really need underpants anyway. It was time for Wallace Head to take charge. To establish control over his own life. To get another notch on his bedpost. By the time this night was over, the notches on my bedpost would number, umm, two. Impressive. That's a 100% increase. You try doing that in one night.

26
Of Great Nutritional Value

I WAS READY TO GO. I was ready for anything.

The doorbell went ding dong ding dong... ding dong ding dong... ding dong ding dong... ding dong ding dong.

That would be Bruce. I had this all under control. I was ready. I opened the door. It was Bruce. And Rosemary. And a tiny blonde woman with disproportionately large bazoombas. I wasn't ready for this. I went to close the door but it was too late. They'd already walked past me.

'Well close the door and come and meet Tania. Gorgeous ain't she? Tania, this is Wally. Don't worry Darl, he always gawks like that when he sees a beautiful woman. Wally, behave mate.'

'Hello Wally,' said Tania. She had a nice smile.

I'd thought it was just going to be Bruce, and that we were going out somewhere, so it had taken me by surprise. Now that I had time to look, I saw that Tania was kind of attractive if you like tiny bottle blondes with very high heels and teensy little waists and really tight red dresses with very large breasts spilling out the top of them. Were there no real breasts left in the world? Was this some sort of disease that had spread throughout the female population? There were Tess's of course, but she wouldn't let me near them anyway, and...

'Wally mate, stop looking down Tania's dress and say hello.'

'Sorry. Tania is it? Charmed I'm sure.' I definitely said. 'That's a lovely red breast,' I thought I may have said.

'Thanks,' said Tania. 'I got them done by Doctor Hung three months ago ... Or did you say dress?'

'Umm. Dress. Or ... umm, not sure, sorry. He does good work everyone says. Umm...'

'Plenty of time for that later you pair,' said Rosemary. 'I'm so dry I could drink a bottle of horse piss. Crack open one of those bottles Brucie.'

I wondered what was in the bottle. I was starting to feel unsure of myself again. Why would anyone want to drink horse piss anyway, and even if they'd wanted to, where would they have bought such a thing? Was it part of this whole kinky sex thing? Masey had never mentioned it. Maybe that's why she'd gone to Bali, or Thailand, or wherever she was. I didn't even know if they had horses there, but if they did...

'Here, get some of this scotch into you mate,' said Bruce, handing me a glass. It looked like horse piss but smelled like scotch. I drank it.

'Another?' he asked, pouring me another.

'No thanks,' I answered, before drinking the second one in a single gulp. 'One's plenty.'

'No worries,' he said, topping up my glass again. 'One it is.'

It was a nice evening. We sat around talking and drank a few drinks. After maybe six drinks the doorbell went ding dong ding dong, and we all stopped talking and looked towards the door. Then the doorbell went ding dong ding dong, and everyone else looked at me, and I looked at everyone else. Then the doorbell went ding dong ding dong, and I said, 'I'll get it.'

Then as I walked towards the door the doorbell went ding dong ding dong, and I opened the door. It was the Thai home delivery guy. 'Order for Missa Head,' he said.

'Ha,' I said, in the triumphant voice of a man who's finally got his shit together and is never going to pay $150 for $104 worth of Thai food ever-a-fucking-gain. 'No way mate. You got the wrong end of the stick this time. Ha.'

'Sorry Wal mate,' said Bruce. 'Forgot to tell you, we rang and ordered it on the way here. You'll have to get it mate, I spent all my cash on the grog.'

'Fine. How much?' I asked, taking out my wallet as Bruce took the food inside.

At least this time I had a twenty.

'One hunnert twenny one dollar.'

I gave him three fifties and slammed the door in his face. It was obviously a conspiracy.

I was seething about these tips.

Seethe, seethe, seethe, I seethed. I was unemployed now. It was quite possible that I couldn't afford this.

Seethe, seethe, seethe.

All this seething was ruining a really nice meal. I decided I needed to stop seething. In a minute. I seethed one bit more. And then another tiny bit. I seethed a final, smooth soothing seethe. It's like a good ejaculation, a nice seethe every now and then, but a bit less sticky. I felt better. I was all seethed out.

'Are you okay?' asked Tania, touching my forearm in such a way that several acres of her breasts were rubbing against me.

'Oh yes,' I said. 'Why do you ask?'

'It doesn't matter,' she said. 'You're very cute Wally. The others have gone upstairs. You were busy muttering about something and didn't notice I expect, but they're gone. And we're alone. So, Handsome. What do you feel like doing?'

I tried to think of something wrong with her. I couldn't, so I just tried to think of anything else. I couldn't. Lack of blood supply to my brain, possibly. She really was a very attractive woman, despite the huge man-made boulders she was lugging around in front of her, and I was a man taking control of his life. I considered whether or not I should try to kiss her, or if perhaps I should wait awhile, maybe have another six drinks while I worked up the courage, or…

Her tongue seemed to have lost something, and it seemed to think the place it had been lost was somewhere a long way down my throat. Her hands seemed to have lost something too, and although it defied logic that if two things had been lost at the same time they'd be lost in two different places, the hands had decided to do their searching down the front of my pants.

I tell you now, what that girl lacked in subtlety and stature, she made up for in efficiency and enthusiasm. My pants were around my ankles before the tongue had made its second quite thorough search of my tonsils, and at that point the tongue must have decided it was barking up the wrong tree and that the hands were probably right after all, because in less than sixty seconds I'd gone from having a nice quiet seethe to having a nice not so quiet slobbering sucking slurping something-or-other being performed on not just Young Wallace, but the entire area of my genitalia.

It was incredible. I tried to stand very still, eyes closed as I didn't wish to cause any embarrassment, but the lack of blood getting to my brain was making it difficult to balance, and besides, it felt like there was more than one person down there, and I was a bit worried Rosemary and Bruce might have sneaked back in and started to help. Opening my eyes, I cast a glance down there, and was quite relieved, yet more than a little amazed, to see just one furiously bobbing blonde head and one pair of extremely overactive hands doing wonders towards shaping my future taste in sexual activity.

'What a beautiful cock,' said Tania, smiling up at me as she took a breath, before filling her mouth again, this time while maintaining eye contact.

'Gnngndthgh,' I may have said, or something very much like it.

It was fantastic. Don't get me wrong, Once in a while, Masey had done … something like this for me, but her few timid licks and kisses for thirty seconds compared to Tania's delightful insightful delicious voracious feasting on eager Young Wallace was as a boiled lolly is to the greatest dessert in the world.

And feast it was … as it turned out, what the hands and the tongue and the cheeks and the lips and the depths of Tania's stretching throat were searching for was obviously of some great nutritional value to her, for she continued to squirm as she sucked and she swallowed, the better to drain every drop from me. It was better than the best seethe a man ever had.

'Wow,' she said.

'Mmmmmmmm,' my throat managed to say.

'Wow. Now that's what I call a cock. Where'd you have it done?' she asked.

'What?' I asked, before staggering sideways, tripping on my pants, which were still around my ankles, and hitting my head on the edge of the coffee table.

27

He Looked at Her with His One Eye

'I THINK you've killed him,' Bruce was saying.

'What a cock,' Tania was saying.

'What a waste,' Rosemary was saying. 'Should I try mouth to cock resuscitation?'

'I think that's what killed him,' Tania was saying. Or maybe I was confused about who was saying what ... there was a loud buzzing noise somewhere in my head, and I couldn't see a thing.

'Maybe I am dead,' I thought I thought.

'Thank fuck for that,' said Bruce. 'You right mate? You've had a fall and hit your head.'

'I think so, but I can't see anything.'

Was I being punished with blindness for watching Tania blow me? See no evil? Maybe I deserved it. And I wasn't even a Catholic. Fuck though. It was so great, it was almost worth blindness.

Bruce was saying ... something ... what?

I floated...

'Wally mate!'

'Yes Bruce?'

'Are you with us Wal? Are you okay?'

'I can't see Bruce.'

'Open your fucking eyes Wal.'

I opened my eyes. Bruce was looking at me.

'Well?' he asked.

'Not particularly,' I said. 'My head hurts. And your nose hairs need trimming.'

'Fuck Wally, you nearly give us a fucken coronary. Anything broken?'

'No,' I said. 'How about you?'

'I need a drink,' said Bruce.

'I want one too,' said Tania.

'Would you like a nice therapeutic blow-job?' asked Rosemary.

My head was still bleeding, but no-one seemed to care. It made me miss the old days, the days of police brutality in this very room. How long had it been? A week? A year? It didn't matter. At least the Tiny Police Force had given me a tea towel to mop up the blood. Correct procedure still counted for something.

'So where'd you have your cock done?' Rosemary was asking.

'Great work isn't it?' piped Tania. 'Not even a trace of a scar from the stitches.'

'W . . . wha . . . what?' I asked them. They were making no sense at all.

'Your beautiful penis,' said Tania. 'Who did the work on it? It's quite the best I've ever seen.'

'Well you did,' I said. 'Didn't you? Or did I dream the whole…?'

'I think they're asking which doctor transplanted a zebra's cock onto you Wally,' said Bruce.

'Yes, who did it Wal? It's wonderful. I can't wait to…'

'Leave him the fuck alone for a minute ladies, can't you see he's confused? Nasty hit on the head, that. You really should stop bleeding all over that rug Wally, it looks expensive. I'll get you a towel mate.'

Clearly, I wasn't well. Also, Young Wallace was still out on display for all to see. And discuss. While Bruce was getting a towel from the bathroom and the women were discussing penises they'd known, I managed to drag myself up onto the lounge and cover Young Wallace with a cushion.

Bruce came back with the towel and suggested to the girls they should go back upstairs with him and leave me to rest, but neither agreed, each suggesting the other two should go upstairs while they themselves would stay here and look after me. This soon led to an argument between them, which started with name-calling and soon degenerated into something more physical.

It certainly made Bruce's eyes light up. Eventually, with the girls worn out from their yelling and scratching and biting at each other, he extricated Rosemary from the tangled mess of heavy breathing and torn clothing, threw her over his shoulder and carried her up the stairs, telling her she'd been a very naughty girl and was about to be severely punished for her behaviour.

Well that was enough for Tania. She tore off what remained of her clothes, and — despite my protests that I was injured and could die — proceeded to pounce upon Young Wallace, who clearly didn't share my concern that the subsequent violent animal acts could injure or kill us, and became, not just a willing participant, but the instigator of what were undoubtedly the depraved acts of a mad-person — or mad-penis as the case may be.

At one point Tania tried to roll a condom onto Young Wallace, but he wasn't having a bar of it.

'They're too small,' she shouted at him. 'You bought the wrong size you dick.' He looked at her with his one eye, but wasn't listening on account of the fact he has no ears.

Over the next few hours, Tania groaned and moaned and complained many times that the various acts of depravity were likely to split her asunder, yet when all was finally quiet, she was still in one piece, and Young Wallace, that stinking slug of depravity, having visited every part of the woman's body it was physically possible to worm his way into, had finally gone to sleep, allowing the blood supply to return to my brain.

And all my poor brain could think of to do, was carve a gigantic Notch Number Two into my metaphorical bedpost.

28
A Debriefing

IT WAS the next day. I was more than a little confused. I felt comprehensively sick and injured. Sick to my stomach, as well as in my stomach. And injured in my head, as well as on it.

The girls had fought again during the night. Apparently Rosemary tried to sneak downstairs for a ride on Young Wallace, but was caught by Tania, who proceeded to hit her with a large vibrator she just happened to have in her handbag. Bruce had tried to break up the fight, suggesting they should all just try to get along, and go upstairs together to make up. But when this heroic suggestion was met with derision, he'd thrown them both out the front door and told them to fuck off home or he'd call the cops. Naturally they complained they had no money for a taxi, but luckily Bruce knew where to find plenty of money. He gave them $100 out of my wallet and told them, 'Thanks, this was fun, let's do it again sometime.'

To which they'd said, 'Fuck you arse-hole,' and run some keys along the paintwork of his ute, which he says happens all the time, and is usually worth it, because after that you never see the crazy bitches again.

So, back to me. Sick. Injured. Confused.

'I don't understand it,' I told Bruce. 'I should feel great. It was incredible. But I feel disgusting. What's wrong with me?'

'Ah Wally,' he said, laughing and shaking his head. 'Ya poor bastard. You never had a one night stand before, I forgot mate. I'll dish us up some brekkie then I'll debrief you mate.'

'I think I was debriefed more than sufficiently by Tania last night,' I said, feeling quite clever, but he ignored me. He was busy admiring the nice even spatter of bacon fat he'd managed to get all over the walls and ceiling of the kitchen.

'Righto Wally,' he said as we sat down to munch on our eggs, bacon, sausages, tomato and baked beans. 'How do you feel?'

'Well, my head and my dick are sore, and my balls ache, and I feel sick to the stomach. But this breakfast is fantastic…'

'Beauty,' he said. 'Welcome to the world of one night stands. That's how you're supposed to feel. Except for the head injury. That's nasty. You're getting quite a collection. Make sure you kick your pants off before you try to walk so it doesn't happen again. And if it does, try to land on a big comfy pair of tits next time.'

'Next time? I can't go through that again. It almost killed me. I feel awful.'

'Yeah, you'll be right once your nut-sack fills back up mate. That huge cock of yours'll be running the show again in no time. You done great mate. How was she, that little Tania? Thought I might get a go after you, but I never managed to talk her around.'

'Ummm...is it...? I mean, is that something men should discuss? I mean...'

'Fuck's sake Wally, it's only a root mate. You're not marrying the woman. So how was she?'

'It was...umm...it was really fucking great actually. I never knew sex could be like that. I never even knew you could do some of those things. Should I call her and ask her out now?'

'Fuck, Wally, settle down mate. Onward and upward eh? There's a whole fucken smorgasbord of women out there. Don't you wanna try a few new dishes? The world's your fucken oyster now mate. You don't wanna restrict yourself to the same meal over and over do you? You just done that for the past thirty years. Spread your wings mate. Time to fly. You're doing great.'

I felt better. Maybe an old dog could learn new tricks after all. Oh, I'd be showing Masey a thing or two when she came back. Then again, what was she learning herself? And who with? I'd show her. I'd learn more ways to make a woman have body-shatteringly intense, delicious, turbulent, agonising, exhausting, violent, all-consuming orgasms than you could poke a vibrator at. Or even read about in some stupid book. Bitch. I'd show her. And when it was done, maybe I'd ask Bruce to cook her some breakfast. It was almost the best part. All those years of muesli with skim milk six days a week, looking forward to your one slice of bacon and one poached egg on two slices of gluten free toast on Sundays. Fuck that dried out shitty excuse for a life. What use is your health if it just keeps you living a miserable life for longer? It was time to burn brighter, and if a bit of fuel added to the fire made it burn out faster, so fucking be it. It was time to start living.

29
They Come in Different Sizes

LIFE WAS looking up, no question about it. I slept the hearty sleep of a man who feels like he's finding his place in the world, and I cruised the internet looking for women, confident as only a man who's just doubled the number of notches on his bedpost can be.

'It ain't enough,' announced Bruce one afternoon when he came in for a chat before doing my lawn. 'You'll go fucken mad mate. You need to work a bit so all the play means something.'

'Are you sure?' I asked. 'I feel great not working. I was made for this life.'

'It's okay for a while,' he said, 'but soon you'll get listless and bored, and no amount of red hot rogering'll be enough.'

'But I hate my job. Besides, they've sacked me. They did put a large pile of money in my account as severance pay though.'

'Must be your lucky day mate,' said Bruce. 'I just happen to be needing a part time offsider to help me with a few lawns, and you just happen to be needing a job. Get your work-boots on Wally, yours needs doing right now.'

I put my white leather running shoes on and followed him outside. It was hot work, and I was sweating like a menopausal woman at the arse end of the Bombay Marathon. Over the next hour I got in trouble six times for doing all sorts of things wrong, but when we walked — that is to say, when Bruce walked, and I staggered — back inside for a drink when it was all over, I felt more like a man than I ever had bossing people around and organising pieces of paper in my prissy office job in the last thirty years.

'That'll be ninety bucks,' said Bruce, holding out one hand while handing me a glass of water with the other.

'I thought it was eighty,' I said.

'Sorry mate,' he said. 'Had to put up my prices. More expenses since I expanded the business with a new employee and all.'

I gave him ninety dollars from my wallet, and he gave me back twenty.

'What's that for?' I asked.

'It's your pay, dickhead. Waddaya reckon it is? You're working now. And there's plenty more where that came from. Nice shoes mate.'

'Thanks,' I said, looking at my brand new runners, now a vibrant shade of *Sir Walter Buffalo blue-tinged green*.

'No worries,' he said. 'By the way, it's Monday, so you're working tomorrow. I'll pick you up at eight. Might wanna bring a big bottle of cold water. Now, let's hit the computer and line up some babes.'

We hit the computer. We were a well-oiled team.

'Waddaya think of this one?' he'd ask.

'Not much,' I'd answer.

'Who fucken asked yer?' he'd ask.

'You did,' I'd answer.

And so it went. Sometimes he'd let me do the online chat to the women, telling me I'd have to learn, that he wouldn't be there to hold my hand forever — but mostly he did the talking. And before you knew it, we were having to decide which of the women to leave out. There just wasn't enough time, or enough condoms as Bruce would say, to go round.

'By the way,' he said at one point, 'you did use a condom with that hot little piece the other night didn't you?'

'Umm … I … I think so.'

'You dopey fuck Wally. You didn't, did you? You stupid fucken dickhead. What the fuck were you thinking? So much for that big cock of yours. Has it started to rot yet?'

'I … I mean, she … I mean, I …'

'Fuck me Wally. Fuck, mate, you'll have to go get it checked out. Good idea anyway. That missus of yours had probably inflicted some horrible pox on you anyway. Better safe than sorry mate. Best get the beggar checked out tomorry eh? Don't worry, you're most likely fine.'

I'd never used condoms with Masey. How was I to know they came in different sizes? But I didn't want to tell Bruce that. I felt like he must finally be thinking I was learning something, and I didn't want to disappoint him.

Woof!

There was a lot a man needed to learn in the world of dating, but I was on a high. Nothing was going to stop me. And soon Masey would be back, maybe, and if she didn't come back? Well, she'd be back. Of course she would.

'So,' said Bruce. 'You done good mate, congratulations. Having considered all the applicants, you came out on top. You got the job. You'll be working two days a week from now on. Tuesday, Wednesday and Friday.'

'That's three days,' I said.

'You must be a mathematical fucken genius,' Bruce said. ' It usually rains one day on average, so Friday's the catch-up day. Got it Einstein?'

'Got it,' I said.

'Yeah, you'll get more than that if you don't remember to wear a condom from now on,' he said. 'See you tomorrow.'

So I worked six hours Tuesday and six hours Wednesday and both days I thought I might die but I didn't. And both days he paid me cash when he dropped me off at home, $120 each day. Twenty bucks an hour. It was the lowest pay I'd earned in years, and the most satisfying I'd earned in my life. And each night I slept like an angel, and woke up feeling like a new person.

And then it was Thursday.

<u>30</u>
You Can't Say Penis in Here

THURSDAY MORNING. Tess day.

A lot had changed in the few days since I'd met her. Back then, less than a week ago, I was an unemployed, naive young fellow who was ready to fall for the first woman who didn't yell obscenities at him and kick him in the testicles with her pointy high heels. But this was the future. A brave new world where a man like me could get all the women he liked—and maybe a few he didn't like—line them up from here to doomsday, bend them all over and service them every which way with his almost certainly slightly bigger than average bald-headed yoghurt-slinger. It was my world now.

Of course, as great as it was, life wasn't perfect. I was out of bacon, sausages, tomatoes, tea, bread, and baked beans, so I ate five fried eggs for breakfast, drank three cups of coffee with varying amounts of sugar, then called Tess.

The phone went brrrt brrrt, brrrt brrrt, brrrt brrrt, then a surprisingly powerful-sounding voice said, 'Therese ... Speak.'

'Umm, Tess? It's, ummm … Wallace … Wallace Head?'

'Wally. Thought you'd forgotten me. Coming for a walk later?'

'Well yes. Yes I am. Ummm … when?'

'I have a few things to do later, so how about six-thirty? Meet you at your place, and we'll go from there okay? Gotta run Wally, bye.'

Excellent. My place. Maybe she did want me after all. A man of the world like Wallace Head might just be getting notch number three on the bedpost before the day was out.

Sure, it would have been nice to go for two women in one night, just to get another one-hundred percent increase in bedpost notches. But this was Tess. Tess!

Ah, the things a man would be prepared to go without, just to have such a woman in his life. A fifty percent increase would just have to do. And again, you try doing that. Mmmm, Tess. Tess.

Mmmm.

In keeping with my status as a new man, and master of his own destiny who could do whatever he liked, I decided to do as Bruce said and go see the doctor to get some tests. No use having a slightly bigger than average single-barrel pump-action sperm-shooter if it was about to rot off from some horrible disease. And besides, now that I'd become a bit of a culinary wizard, I needed to shop too. From a list. A list! I wrote it on the only piece of paper I could find.

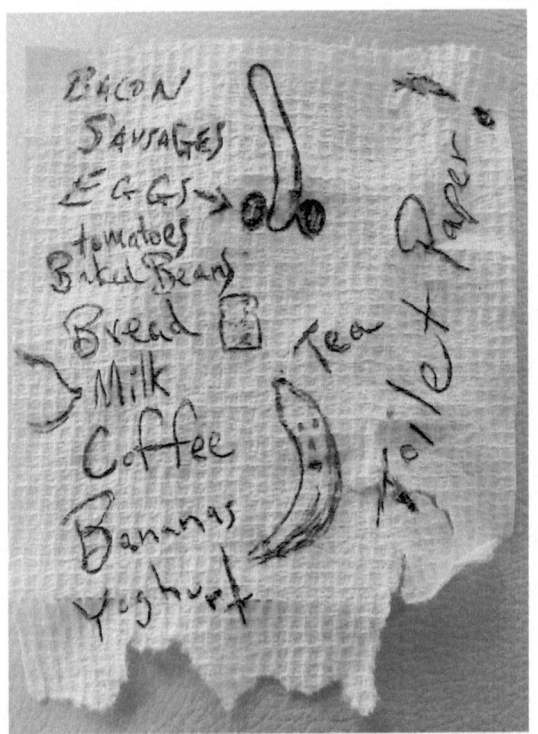

The toilet paper on the list wasn't for eating. Just saying. Me being a culinary wizard and all, you might have been wondering. Toilet paper's useful for many things — including writing your shopping list on — but it's not for eating. Although I've noticed that if there's any women around it disappears at a rate of at least one roll per woman per day, but when there's only men it hardly disappears at all.

So maybe they do eat it. Women I mean. Bruce says they do. Or maybe they just steal it. Or unroll it and flush it down the dunny because they have shares in the toilet paper company. Not sure. Just saying. I'd ask someone, but last time I asked I got hit.

I drove to the shops. I parked in the car park. Well, it's where you park. I went first to see the doctor. It was one of those fancy new medical centres, full of glass and shiny tiles and a few sick people sitting around the waiting room trying to cough all over you. I went to the reception desk. A very large, extremely beautiful girl with a magnificent hooked nose asked, 'How can I help you?'

I said, 'I want to see a doctor. Why else would I be here?'

She said, 'You might be here to fix the plumbing.'

I said, 'Is it broken?'

She said, 'No it isn't. You don't look sick. What's wrong with you?'

I said, 'I might have something wrong with my penis. Does it make any difference?'

She said, 'Not to me. Anyway, you shouldn't really say penis in here. You're upsetting people.'

I looked around. A few people did look a little upset. 'Well, you asked me. So what should I say instead?'

She said, 'You should make something up, I suppose. Say there's something wrong with your nose maybe instead. Be a bit less offensive, wouldn't it?'

'Fine then,' I said. 'There might be something wrong with my nose.'

'What's wrong with it?' she asked.

'I stuck it in every single orifice of a sex-crazed woman without putting a condom on it first,' I told her.

'Oh,' she said. 'Well you should go to the medical centre next door then. This is a solicitor's office.'

I left without thanking her, or meeting the stares of the people in the waiting room. I went next door to the medical centre. It looked pretty much the same. Even the girl behind the reception desk looked the same. Like, exactly the same. Very large, and with a magnificent hooked nose. Two rare beauties in one day. I only hoped this one would be nicer to me. She was on the phone. I waited. 'Really?' she was saying. 'Really? What a fucking dickhead. Unbelievable. And what did you say?' She looked down her magnificent nose at me like she'd put in an order for me, someone had brought me to her, and I'd turned out to be a vomit, when what she'd been expecting was a strawberry and cream pie. 'Fucking unbelievable. Okay, see you tonight.' She just looked at me. For a while.

'How can you help me?' I asked. It may have been the wrong thing to say.

She just shook her head and didn't help me. Her eyes wandered from my face to my pants then back again. 'First time here?' she asked.

'Yes,' I said, glad she was finally helping.

'Fill in these forms.'

I filled in the forms. Standard stuff.

Name — Wallace Head.

Address — 1 Quiet Street, Wealthyville.

Medical history — I barely had one. The possibility of a rotting redheaded rooster was about the most exciting thing that had ever happened to me.

Reason for Visit — Hmmm. What to write? Possible penis problem didn't seem to be the right thing to write, especially after what had gone on next door. And the receptionist was watching me with a mean look in her eyes — I decided to leave it blank.

I folded the form so she couldn't see I'd left a question unanswered, and handed it back to her. She unfolded it, looked down her nose at me and pointed to the unanswered question.

'Reason for Visit!' she didn't quite scream. Everyone stopped coughing to watch what would happen.

'Ummm ... I ... need to see a doctor?' I replied hopefully.

'Obviously,' she said. 'Then she spoke very quietly and deliberately, and I had to lean closer to her so I could hear properly. 'This, Mister Head, is a medical centre. You need to use your tiny little brain, and fill in the tiny little form so we know which doctor you need to see. And you don't go next door instead of in here and tell my sister and a room full of people your cock's about to rot off because you've been sticking it in some skinny rich bitch's fucking arse-hole!'

'Ah,' I said. 'You have a lovely sister. Lovely girl. Very attractive. Are you twins?'

She wrote STD test on the form in large angry letters that threatened to tear the paper, then said, 'Mister Head. Just because my sister and I are overweight doesn't mean we don't have feelings. You're an absolute disgrace.'

'No no no no no no no no no no no no no,' I said, waving my hand at least once for every no. 'I never implied that you were.'

'Were what?' she asked. I was pretty sure I was about to be hit.

'Were, ummm, nothing. I mean, I ... I mean, you and your sister are most attractive young ladies. As I was just saying.'

'Don't patronise me,' she said. 'Please go and sit down.'

I didn't know what to do. I'd never meant to upset them. It was their own fault. We'd obviously got off on the wrong foot, I thought. 'We've obviously got off on the wrong foot,' I said.

'Just please sit down sir,' she said in a voice possibly designed to make me feel sorry for being mean to her.

I had to do something. I had to make it up to her. To both of them. Money. I'd give them money, I thought.

A nice night on the town. 'How about a nice night out on the town,' I heard me say.

'What? Who do you mean?' she asked.

'You and your sister,' I said. 'I'll pay.'

'You fucking arse-hole,' she said. 'We're not prostitutes you can buy you sick fuck.'

'No, I meant ... No, I didn't mean ... I just wanted to treat you both to a...'

'You want to take us out? Because if that's not what you're saying, I'll...'

'Yes,' I rushed into saying, a bit before I heard me say it, and a while before I realised what I'd done.

She looked at me like she'd caught me looking down her top, and said, 'Fine then. But no funny business. Friday night. And find a friend to come with us. This isn't some sick two sisters on one rich old fucker thing. Do you even have any friends?'

'Of course I have one,' I said. 'He's a very good friend. His name's Bruce.'

'Don't give a fuck if his name's Wilbur the talking pig,' she said. 'And don't think you'll be fucking me with that diseased little cock of yours either. Now go with Doc Harrison here and get your knob checked.'

She handed the forms to the doctor. He was at least a hundred years old, seemed to be completely deaf, and wore a herringbone suit he'd obviously had on for a good thirty years or more. I followed him, really very slowly, wondering if the automobile had yet been invented when he became a doctor, whether they even had to pass a test to become a doctor back then, and whether he'd actually die of old age before he managed to get to wherever we were going. But eventually we made it all the way down the short hallway and into a room on the right.

'What's the problem?' asked the doc in a creaky old man voice.

'Nothing I reckon.'

'Been forgetting to wear a glove on the old tallywacker eh?' he said, looking at the form and laughing a creaky old man laugh.

'Just the once,' I said. 'Mostly.'

'Right you are,' he said. 'Right. Brace yourself then, young fella, and we'll get it all checked out for you.'

I dropped my pants to the floor and stood there, as vulnerable as a man ever could be without bending over, waiting for him to turn around and inflict whatever horror it was that doctors inflicted on possibly disease carrying willies. I hadn't thought this through. Maybe I could run. But the pants around the ankles thing was stopping me. I couldn't afford another hit on the head. Slowly, he turned around. And there, in his hands, was the biggest fucking needle I ever saw.

31
The Right Number of Hands

'SILLY YOUNG FUCKER,' Doc Harrison was saying. 'Just fainted. What he was doing with his tallywacker out I'll never know. I had the needle in my hand to take some blood from him, and it must have stuck him when I tried to save him from falling. Dopey young coot. Got blood all over my good fucking suit.'

'Never mind,' a lovely soft voice was saying. 'You go and rest Doctor Harry, I'll get the needle out of him and clean up in here. Ah, you're awake,' she said. 'You gave Dr Harry quite a scare.'

'I gave him a scare? Me? He was going to put that huge needle down my dingle-dangle! He should be locked up.'

'Nonsense Mister Head,' she said. 'Please calm down or I'll call the police. He was merely going to take blood from you. And why, may I ask, are you lying around in here exposing your enormous willy-wacker for all the world to see? You're lucky I didn't trip over it just now when I came into the room.'

It was true. I was wearing no pants. My head hurt, and there was a large needling sticking out of me just above my right ear. I may have slightly misunderstood the situation. I didn't know what to say, so I said that. That I didn't know what to say.

The doctor was a woman, much younger than me, Indian. 'That's okay,' she said. 'Happens all the time.' And the sexy-voiced little bitch pulled the needle out of my skull.

'Aaaaaaaaarrrrrrrrrrgggghhhhh!' I said.

She applied a dressing to the hole in my head, held twelve fingers up in front of my eyes, and asked me 'How many fingers?'

'It's my poor whatsy-wicker I'm more worried about,' I told her.

She rolled six of her eyes, got a fresh needle, took blood from three of my arms, put dressings on all the wounds, told me, 'Please put your enormous willy-wacker back in your pants before leaving,' and made me sign several forms at once. Luckily I had the right number of hands with the right number of pens in them.

'Don't forget to call me,' said the receptionist as I walked past her on my way out. She seemed to have become even fatter since I last saw her.

32
The Most Handsome Man in the World

I MANAGED to get to the grocery store without incident. It took me a few goes to get the coin into the trolley lock so I could use it, but I eventually managed. My list wasn't much help to begin with, but after a few minutes my sight returned to normal, and I did the shopping.

I got everything on the list, plus some cheese. Plenty of cheese. Cheese slices with plastic, cheese slices without plastic. Sticks of cheese. Round packets of fruity cheese. Wedges of blue cheese, and wedges of not blue cheese. Gouda cheese, and not so gouda cheese. Cheese.

It cost $152.50. Just my luck, I thought. I handed over four fifties and started to walk away. 'Excuse me sir,' said the little girl who ran the shop, or maybe just that checkout. 'Your change.'

She gave me $47.50. 'Really?' I asked. I could have kissed her. Luckily I didn't. I would have gotten myself arrested. She was about fourteen.

I went back to the car, put groceries in it, left the trolley in the middle of the car park so some kid could take it back and get the dollar out of it. Gotta teach the little shits private enterprise somehow. Then I drove home, and somewhat impressively remembered to put all the shopping away. Even the cheese.

I'd turned into a totally efficient homebody. I was organised. I was healthy. There was food in the fridge and enough dunny paper to survive the visits of twelve women or every man I'd ever met in the bathroom. I mean ... not men I'd met in the bathroom. I don't meet men in bathrooms. That'd be, umm, gay. Not that there's anything wrong with that. I mean the food was in the fridge and the toilet paper was in the bathroom ... but no men. Efficient, that was me. And I still had an hour before Tess would arrive. I busied myself having a shower and putting on clean clothes. Well, I would have put on clean clothes if I'd had any. Nobody had washed them, so I put on the ones that didn't smell as bad as the others, and sat out the front on a lawn chair trying to look interesting and prosperous and like I knew what was going on.

Tess arrived early.

'Would you like some cheese?' I asked. 'I have seven different kinds you know.' If that didn't tell her I knew what was going on, nothing would.

'Hi Wally,' she said. 'You've hurt your head again I see. Are you okay?'

'Fit as a fiddle,' I replied, with all the confidence a man of the world can muster even though he's been pushed around by fat twins and stabbed in the head earlier in the day. 'Fit as a fiddler's fiddle. Fit as a fiddler's fiddle when he's having a fiddle. Fit as a...'

'Wally!'

'Yes Tess?'

'Let's go.'

We walked down my leafy street, around a leafy corner into the next leafy street, and down to the huge leafy park people like to walk around.

We walked around.

Actually, we talked around too.

Bruce had taught me to always begin with small talk. 'That's a really small dog,' I said.

'It's a fully grown Golden Retriever,' said Tess.

'But it's small for a fully grown one. And its owner's quite small.'

'Right,' she said. 'So Wally, I believe the deal was that we'd meet once a week, and while we walked you'd tell me who you are.'

'Exactly!' I said.

We walked a bit further.

'Well?'

'Well what?' I asked. Two could play at this game.

'So who are you Wally?'

'Does that matter Tess?'

'Only if it matters to you Wally. You don't have to

tell me you know. You don't even have to think about it. It's your life. We can turn around, go back to your place, and…'

…make mad passionate love, she didn't say. Although her not saying it still seemed to fill my ears and my brain, at least what was left of my brain after all the recent knocks and stabs I'd taken to the head.

'Sorry,' I said. 'Go back to my place and do what did you say?'

'Go our separate ways Wally. Say goodbye, it's been nice knowing you. So, is that your choice?'

'No! No Tess, it isn't.'

'Look,' she said. 'I like you Wally. You're a nice man, and I think you're a decent one, if a little misguided at the moment, and I'll be a friend to you. And as a friend, I'm telling you, you need to find out who you are. That's why I agreed to meet with you once a week. The process of telling me, once a week, who you are, will make you think about it. And you'll grow, really you will. Who you are will change over time. It's not a test. I'll never be your girlfriend, I'll never sleep with you. There's no reason to lie to me or do anything to impress me. So just tell me. Wallace Head. Who are you today?'

Okay, I thought, and took a breath. 'Okay,' I said, and took another one. 'I'm Wally now, not Wallace. Maybe I always was Wally, somewhere deep down, but I was too

good at being who I was told to be. But today, I'm Wally.'
I looked at her, hoping I was doing it right.

'That's great Wally,' she said. 'Wonderful. Tell me more.'

It made me warm, me talking about this, and Tess actually listening. It was like she really did care, and it was hard not to be falling in love with her instead of telling her who I was, but I worked at it.

'Okay. I'm somebody who doesn't want to work behind a desk any more, never not ever again. I'm someone who enjoys working outside, mowing lawns in the dust and the heat, and who feels like the work he now does gives him more than just money. Which is good, because it doesn't bring in much of that.'

'You're mowing lawns? Fascinating. What else Wally?'

'I'm someone who some women are actually interested in going out with. Plenty of women.'

'Oh yes, do tell Mister Gigolo,' she said.

'Well, your friend Rosemary…'

'She's not my friend!'

'Sorry, your *neighbour* Rosemary brought a friend to visit last Saturday night. I thought she'd have told you.'

'I've managed to avoid her all week. And?'

'Well, she and her friend Tania came to visit and Tania took quite a shine to me, actually.'

'Yes I'm sure. Too much information Wallace.'

'My name's Wally now.'

'Right. Sorry. Wally. So what happened?' She'd stopped, and was inspecting the bottom of her shoes for chewing gum or something.

'Too much information, you said. So…?'

'It's fine if you don't want to tell me.' She was walking fast now and I had trouble keeping up. 'But there's no reason not to, we're just friends after all. I mean, whatever Wal.'

'Well,' I said, 'she kissed me and stuff, then she just kind of attacked me, and it was so great, and then I fell and hit my head here, see? And then I must have been knocked out for a bit, and Bruce and Rosemary must have come downstairs and we were all talking about stuff, then Bruce carried Rosemary back up the stairs, then Tania came at me again, and I told her not to because I thought I might die, but she still did and I didn't.'

'Oh. Didn't what?'

'Die. I didn't die.'

'Right. So you had sex with this Tinea woman then?'

'Well, I don't like to brag or anything, but I was totally fantastic!'

'Disgusting,' she said. 'And you'd just met her. I'm sorry Wallace, but I thought you were better than that.'

'Wally. My name's Wally now. That's who I am, remember? It was you who said it was important. It was you who said to find out who I am. And to tell you. And now I'm telling you, and you're just getting angry with me. I'll never understand women. And you eat all the toilet paper.'

'You idiot,' she said. We walked awhile without talking.

'That's a small dog,' she said after about five minutes.

'It's that same Golden Retriever,' I said.

'Yes,' she said. 'But now its owner's pants are inside out, and his John Thomas is hanging out of his fly.'

'Really?' I said, straining my eyes to see if his John Thomas was bigger than mine.

'No Wally. I was pulling your leg. Bit slow sometimes aren't you? Good thing you're the most handsome man in the world isn't it?'

'I am?'

'Oh dear. No Wally, you're not. Pulling your leg again. You'll learn. But you're alright.'

'Really? I mean…'

'Yes, really,' she said. 'You look good and you're a decent man. I'm sorry Wally, about before I mean. You're right of course. You need to find out who you are, and it's going to take a while, and you're going to do many things, and some will be smarter than others. I hope you at least had the sense to wear a condom,' she said.

'Of course I did,' I told her. At least she didn't ask me who stabbed me in the head, or why. My lying skills are not quite all they could be.

33
Sisters You Say?

EVEN THOUGH it was Friday and it hadn't rained any days this week, Bruce still let me mow lawns with him. We only had three to do though, and that was good he said, because he reckoned I needed a bit more training.

Woof!

So after we finished we went back to my place, drank coffee, ate cheese and fired up the computer. He decided that this time he wouldn't take over too much, and just watch me chat to some women.

'But don't commit to nothing,' he said. 'We've already got some lined up for tonight, and if it goes good we'll keep them all weekend. It'll be like a long term relationship, waddaya reckon mate!'

'Oh,' I said. 'I've lined us up a couple of nice young ladies too Bruce.'

'Good work Wally, I'm impressed mate. Young stuff eh? What are we talking? Forty?'

'Umm... mid to late twenties maybe. I didn't ask them their age. Am I allowed to ask?'

'Ask anyone anything you want mate. You got rights,

same as anyone. Worst they'll do is hit you when they see you. What age did it say on their profiles Wal mate? Not that it means much, we're most of us lying about our age on the dating sites.'

'Oh, they're not from the internet. I met them when I went to the doctor. Sisters they are.'

'Fair dinkum Wally, you're flying mate. So you actually got phone numbers for these young girlies? Probably bullshit, they're pulling your leg mate. Did you try the number?'

'Not yet. But why would they lie Bruce? I promised we'd take them to dinner.'

'Unbelievable. So when's this dinner mate?'

'Ummm. Tonight?'

'Right,' said Bruce, rolling his eyes and shaking his head. Usually only women did that at me, so I waited quietly, hoping he'd only complain and not hit me. 'So, let's just run through this together Wal mate. Tonight, we've organised to meet the new women we've been chatting up on the net all week up the pub at 8.30 for a few drinks, then hopefully bringing them back here to play kinky games all weekend. But you've also organised for us to be going out, to dinner no less, with two women you met while you were visiting the pox-doctor? How the fuck is that gonna work mate?'

'But I promised!'

'Are they hot? Not saying you done the wrong thing Wally. If they're young and hot, we'll forget the others and do them instead. So? Blondes? Brunette? Sisters you say. Fucking kinky prick you.'

'Well, they're, ummm ... they're very alike. Twins I think. And they have, ummm, well their, I mean they have huge...'

'Huge tits? Arses? Fuck Wally, spit it out mate, what are they like, we gotta decide, time to shit or get off the pot.'

'Big noses. They have big noses Bruce. Huge. Enormous. Biggest noses I ever saw. And I'm scared of them.'

'Scared of their noses? Yer fucken mad Wally. What are you scared of? Nothing wrong with big noses mate. Horny. Get it Wally? Fucken horny mate. Noses? Horns? No? Forget it. So, hot young girls with big noses then, yeah?'

'Ummm...'

'What ain't you telling me Wal? Something here's not adding up. What is it?'

'Well ... they're slightly ... rotund.'

'Ro fucking tund? Ro fucking tund? As in rows of fucking tonnage? Fucking fatties? With big fucking noses? You sick bastard Wally. Huge tits too?'

'Ummm. I suppose. I mean, I didn't really...'

'Call now mate. We need to know before tonight. Maybe we'll feed the fatties up at dinnertime, fill em up with a couple of cock-burgers, roll em down the street and still get to the pub in time to get the others as well. Unless they're all up for some girl on girl into the bargain. Never know our luck mate, not since they all started on these books. Sky's the limit. By the way, did you get that rope? This Sandy and Mandy we're meeting at the pub, they're interested in trying the rope, and I told em you're a fucken expert at it.'

'I forgot to put it on my shopping list. And I didn't see any at the supermarket either.'

'No worries mate. Well let's forget the computer for the day, we got too many women for now anyway, and we'll go get some rope from the rock climbing place. But first, call and line up the fatties.'

I took my phone out of my pocket and placed it on the desk. I went through my other pockets trying to find the number of the girl from the medical centre. I didn't even know her name. I couldn't find a piece of paper with her name on it.

'I can't find her number Bruce,' I said.

'Did you put it into your phone,' he asked.

'No.'

'So she gave you a piece of paper with it on?'

'No.'

'Did she give you her fucking number or not Wally?'

'Maybe she didn't.'

'So you made the whole thing up you dick?'

'No.'

'Fuck Wally, did you organise to take these women out or not? I may have to kill you. Don't make me whip your arse with the whipper snipper again. Funniest fucken thing I ever saw.'

'She said … she said don't forget to call her. At work! She means at work!'

'Right. About fucken time Einstein. Call her.'

I called the medical centre. The phone went brrrt brrrt, brrrt brrrt, brrrt brrrt, brrrt brrrt, then it stopped going brrrt brrrt, and a familiar voice said, 'Leafy Suburb Medical Centre, how can I help you?'

I said, 'Hello.'

The voice said, 'How can I help you?'

I said, 'You already said that.'

The voice said, 'You're that troublemaker from yesterday aren't you?'

I said, 'Maybe I am and maybe I'm not. Do you mean the troublemaker who got stabbed in the head by an ancient doctor?' Bruce rolled his eyes at that one. I hadn't yet told him. What happens at the medical centre stays at the medical centre.

She said, 'Ha. Thought you wouldn't be game to call. You can pick us up from here at six-thirty. And you'd better take us somewhere fancy. And your friend better be a real person and not some weird puppet or something. Okay, I'm going, bye.'

I said, 'Busy eh?'

She said, 'No, not at all. You're just boring and annoying and I don't want to talk to you. Don't be late.' She hung up, and the phone went beep beep beep beep beep beep beep beep beep beep beep beep beep beep beep. Then Bruce took it off me, shaking his head again.

34
To Happy Marriages

WE WENT to the indoor climbing gym. There we bought a thirty metre length of rope, purple, an automatic belay device called a grigri, grey, some locking carabiners, red, and two adjustable climbing harnesses, also red.

'I thought we were just getting rope,' I said.

'Better idea,' Bruce said. 'You're gonna fucken love this mate. You'll be thanking me later. Now pay the man.'

It cost four hundred dollars, and I didn't know what it was for. Luckily I'd worked this week, and made three hundred. It was probably my turn to roll my eyes and shake my head, but I didn't think of it at the time, and later, when I did, it was far too late to do so without explaining why. So I didn't. I'm probably no good at it anyway. Although I've seen plenty of other people do it, and it doesn't look that hard.

We bought some alcohol to get us through the weekend too. Almost three hundred dollars worth. It was a lot of alcohol, considering neither of us drink much. Pay the man, I expected Bruce to say. 'Put your wallet away mate,' Bruce actually did say.

Bruce needed clothes, so we went to his place. I'd never been there, didn't even know where it was. It was about twenty minutes drive from my place. From my leafy suburb, we drove through another leafy suburb, then through a busy concrete suburb, a mostly leafy suburb and into a bushy suburb. Then we drove through that to the bushiest end of the bushiest street, and at the end of the road through an open gate down a dirt driveway to an old corrugated iron shed.

'Home,' he said as we stopped. 'Well come on, you better have the guided tour.'

Well, it was only a shed from the front, which it turned out was really the back. We walked along the side, which was the, umm, side … and around the back, which was really the front, and then I saw it wasn't only an old corrugated iron shed at all. It was beautiful big yellow mud bricks and huge timber posts, massive timber beams everywhere, and floor to ceiling windows looking out over a wilderness of trees, rocks and a glimpse of water at the bottom of the valley.

'Well, that's it pretty much,' he said as we walked inside. 'Solar power. Tank water. A roof over my head. Share it with the possums at night and the birds in the daytime. My shed.'

'It doesn't quite face the view properly Bruce. It's a bit … sideways.'

'Faces true north mate. Passive solar, you know? Gets the sun inside it in the winter and heats the place up, but the vines grow over the pergola and keep the sun right out in summer. Cluey bugger my old dad.'

It was one big room and the pergola. And the toilet was outside, just sitting there on the deck facing the valley. It was a shock to the system. To know someone who lived like this. It was a shed in the bush. With the toilet and the shower outside. In the bush.

Bruce grabbed some clothes from the bedroom ... the bed-corner ... some timber shelves near his bed ... and said, 'Cat got yer tongue mate? Not as fancy as you're used to is it?'

'I've never seen anything like it,' I told him.

It was the truth. I never had. And it was making me feel ... different. Calm. But excited. Different. Better.

'Well we can't all live like the royals Wally. Belonged to my parents. All I managed to retrieve from my divorce settlement, and I had to get a mortgage just to keep it. I used to love it here you know. Let's go mate. Depresses the shit outta me now.'

'It's ... so quiet here. I like it,' I said, as we drove out onto the street.

'Too quiet. Just a sad fucken hole now mate.'

'But you must like living here Bruce. It's so...'

'Don't wanna talk about it Wally,' he said, pulling his

hat down over his eyes and snuggling into the leather upholstery of the Lexus.

'But it…'

'Fucken shoosh mate. I'm trying to have a nap.'

And that was that. It troubled me as I drove, the way Bruce was. He had this amazing place, you could see it was all handmade, the bricks and the timber and even most of the furniture, the more I thought about it the lovelier I realised it was, and it should have been such a comfort and a pleasure to him, and it just wasn't. I thought of Bruce being happy before, when he was still married, then not happy, then really not happy, the way it had all slipped away from him. I thought of Tess, asking me to tell her who I am, and then I thought of Masey, and how unhappy she always was the last few years, and angry sometimes too, and I wondered if it was my fault or if it was nobody's fault, the way these things go in the end.

Then soon enough, or too soon, or at about the right time, we were back at my house, and Bruce stopped pretending to be asleep and we went inside, had two drinks, one each that was, then another two drinks, and on the second one Bruce raised his glass and said, 'To happy marriages, Wally.' And as we touched glasses, I saw into Bruce's eyes. And though I already knew he was a good friend, and a good person, the thing I only found out today, was I really hadn't known him at all.

35
Why, Hello My Lovelies

I WAS out of clean socks now too, but it was okay, I'd remembered what I used to do before I married Masey. Just turn your socks inside out. And undies were a thing of the past, I hadn't bothered with them for days. Free and happy. Happy and free.

When I came out of the bathroom Bruce told me I looked ridiculous, and tried to march me upstairs to choose better clothes.

'There's no clothes up there,' I protested.

'Waddaya mean there's no clothes up there? Course there is. Fucken mad,' he said, shaking his head again.

'They're all in the laundry,' I said, 'apart from these, which aren't as stinky as the others.'

'They're dirty?'

'Yes.'

'Why are they dirty Wally?'

'Well hello?' I said, just like I'd heard some obviously brilliant teenagers say it. 'Nobody washed them.'

'Right. You don't know how to use a washing machine, do you?'

'Well, I…'

'Fucken dumb-arse.' He started throwing some of my clothes into the machine and the others into two piles, saying stuff like, 'Colour, white, colour, dark, white, white, dark, colour.' Then he showed me how to put detergent in the machine and turn it on.

'Well that's easy,' I said.

'Well fucken do it next time,' he said. 'Stinky prick.'

We went outside and Bruce drove us to the medical centre in my Lexus. The girls were waiting out the front for us.

'That's them,' I said.

'They're fucking gorgeous,' he said as he pulled over.

'Hello, how's Doctor Harry today?' I said to the one I thought was the one from the medical centre.

'Which one do you think I am?' she asked me.

'You're the one from the medic…'

'You don't even know our names do you? You shouldn't refer to people as The One From Wherever and all that. It's disrespectful. You'll upset people,' she said. I knew then she was the one from the solicitors office. I'd have known that You Shouldn't from anywhere.

'I'm sorry,' I said. 'Won't happen again. This is my friend, Bruce.'

'Why hello my lovelies,' said Bruce. 'Wally said you were both pretty, but he did you no justice, none whatsoever.

What's your names then?'

'Marisa', 'Larissa', they said, or maybe it was 'Larissa', 'Marisa,' it was all so overlapped I couldn't quite tell which name came out of which mouth. All I knew was they'd swapped clothes since I last saw them, and they seemed to have become even fatter.

'Wally dear chap,' said Bruce.

'Yes Bruce?'

'Do be a gentleman and open the door for the lovely ladies will you please, there's a good fellow.'

'Certainly old chap,' said I, wondering why we were speaking this way.

I got out and held open the door for the lovely ladies, and they started pushing and pulling at each other's clothes, both trying to be the one to sit in the front next to Bruce. Well they weren't both gonna fit … What these girls needed was their own postcode. One each.

36
Within Harpooning Distance

'Fancy car,' said Larissa or Marisa, whichever one was in the front.

'Thanks,' said Bruce. 'Nothing beats driving a gorgeous young lady in a fancy car.'

'Hee hee, ha ha, hee hee,' went Marisa and Larissa.

'Except driving two gorgeous young ladies in a fancy car,' he said.

'Hee hee, ha ha, hee hee,' went Larissa and Marisa.

It was hardly fair. It was my car after all. I decided to set things straight. About the car I mean. 'You know, I really should…'

'Exactly,' said Bruce. 'You really should have booked the restaurant Wally. We're a bit too late to get into a really classy place tonight, but next time we'll go somewhere better ladies, I promise. Wally's sorry, aren't you mate?'

'Well yes, but I probably should…'

'Don't worry Wally, I'm sure the girls won't mind Thai food tonight. Great Thai food round the corner ladies, have you been there? Very nice indeed.'

'Oh yes,' said Larissa or Marisa, whichever one was

taking up most of the back seat. 'Lovely, isn't it? Thai's fine, isn't it Sis?'

'Just this once,' said Sis, the one in the front.

Bruce parked and we walked to the restaurant, the girls walking each side of Bruce, all arm-in-arm, and me walking behind. They took up the whole footpath, and cars had to steer out towards the middle of the road to get around Marisa or Larissa's huge fat arm and shoulder and chest and belly and arse-cheek, which were all doing this big side-wobble sort of thing and encroaching on the road. I didn't mind being left out. I didn't much like Larissa. Or Marisa for that matter. Whichever one they were.

We arrived at the restaurant and went in, single file. Not saying they were fat, that's just how doors work, you have to go through one at a time usually. Although they were quite fat. No, not really. They were humongous. The little Thai guy behind the counter looked nervous. Maybe he thought they were going to eat him. I was being really careful to not say anything, in case I said what I thought, instead of what I thought I should say.

'Give us your best table for four Garcon,' said Bruce.

'Sorry Misser, all book out. Come back tomorrow or get takeaway now,' said the guy. He looked at Marisa and Larissa, who were looking menacingly hungry. 'Plenty takeaway. Plenty. Lots.'

'How about it ladies? Some fine takeaway, and back home for a couple of drinks around the pool. How does that sound?'

'Sounds lovely Bruce,' said Marisa or Larissa while the other one smiled adoringly in Bruce's direction.

I never saw two girls order so much food, and Bruce was only encouraging them. We waited while they cooked it, and I amused myself by watching the chairs Marisa and Larissa were sitting on. Somehow they survived the ordeal, but I wouldn't have liked to have been the next person to sit on them. There's only so much punishment ordinary metal can take. The food was ready, I was allowed to pay of course, and Marisa or Larissa called me a cheapskate because I waited for my two dollars change from the hundred-and-fifty I handed over. I was just happy to get change. At least I was having a good run with change. First at the grocery store, then here. Things were really going my way.

Bruce drove us back to my place and we went inside. Those girls could eat. Those girls could really eat. And fast. There were no leftovers, and I was still hungry. They were no slouches with the alcohol either. By the end of dinner they were finishing the third bottle of wine, and just beginning to get tipsy.

I wasn't drinking. Bruce had devised a plan: if things were going well with Larissa and Marisa, he'd stay here and keep them entertained, and I'd go to the pub and meet up with Sandy and Mandy. My mission was to meet them, not fuck it up, and try to get them to come back here by fair means or foul. I didn't really understand what that meant, but Bruce seemed to have confidence in me, and I didn't want to seem stupid by asking.

Halfway into the second bottle of scotch, Bruce suggested a swim.

'We don't have our bathing suits,' said Marisa or Larissa.

'That's why I suggested it,' said Bruce. 'You see ladies, I'm what you might call a connoisseur. I appreciate fine women, and you two young ladies are, to coin a phrase, smokin!'

I couldn't believe it, but it actually worked. Almost all their clothing fell off, and they jumped into the pool in the finest exhibition of the synchronised belly-buster I've ever been unfortunate enough to witness. The level of water in the pool went up then the level of the water in the pool went down. Up because their enormous bulk was displacing so much water, down because the splash resulted in a huge quantity of water being thrown out of the pool and over the neighbours' fence. I thought I heard their dog yelp but I couldn't be sure. I hoped I was wrong. Even if the splash hadn't been enough to drown it, the force could have killed it, or the wave might have washed it away. Not that

I really much cared. Never did like that dog. Yappy little shit.

'What are you looking at?' asked Marisa or Larissa.

Very large ocean-dwelling creatures in what suddenly looks like a very small swimming pool, I thought, and was very glad to realise I hadn't said it. I smiled my most winning smile instead of speaking, and hoped beyond hope they thought the smile was genuine.

'Does he have to be here?' Larissa or Marisa asked Bruce.

'Yeah, he's creepy and diseased,' said Marisa or Larissa, 'can't he just leave?'

Bruce didn't seem to quite know what to do. Obviously torn between his desire to have some sort of weird interspecies sex romp with the whales now inhabiting the pool and his desire to keep being my friend, he whispered, 'Fuck off to the pub and pick up the other sheilas Wally.'

Then, with a roar of excitement, he told every neighbour within whale harpooning distance, 'I'M GOIN IN!' And with that he tore off every stitch of his clothing and jumped arse-first into the pool.

I went inside to find some more food, turning for a final look at Bruce just in case he didn't survive the horror he was obliviously rushing towards. At least if he didn't survive — and the possibility seemed unlikely — I'd have a fond last memory of him doing something he loved. Last I saw of him, he was drowning in a tittie sandwich that was so gargantuan it could have fed the population of a good-sized fishing village for a month.

I bolted down a can of cold baked beans, walked out to the Lexus and drove to the pub.

It was going to be an interesting challenge.

37
Secret Women's Business

I WAS EARLY. My clothes were a bit stinky, but even in pubs close to nice leafy suburbs, there's always something stinkier to disguise the smell of your clothes.

The place was pretty full, so I went to my usual position down the back. When I say usual position, I really mean only position, as I'd only been here once before. When Masey was still around, we *never liked pubs*, so I'd never been in here. She, I mean we, no fuck it, I definitely mean she, may have had a point though. They're loud and they stink, and there's a lot of people in them being drunken louts and acting tough while they try to impress the opposite sex, or sometimes the same sex. And the men are even worse.

So I went up the back to my spot, and luckily there was nobody there, possibly on account of there being a bit of a vomit-smell, most likely emanating from that bit of a damp looking patch on the carpet, or possibly from a few interestingly coloured particles on the wall.

Some people looked at me a bit, which I thought might be a bad sign, or a good sign, or not a sign at all, and I thought I may perhaps have looked a bit odd just sitting there alone in my not quite stinky enough for a pub clothes, so I went to the bar and bought myself two large beers, one with low alcohol and one with high alcohol. Then I went back to my spot, and nobody was there again, so I sat one beer down in front of me and the other in front of where someone else would have been sitting if they'd been there with me, and then it only looked like I was there with someone who'd gone to the toilet.

So I drank my beer as slowly as I could, but after a while the glass was empty, and by then it would have looked to other people like I was either pretending to be there with somebody, or that whoever I was there with had gone to the toilet and had been in there a really long time doing a really enormous shit, which I didn't really like, so I swapped the glasses over and then it looked like the other person had just gone to the toilet, and I'd just returned from doing a really enormous shit, which I thought wasn't so bad.

So when I was halfway through the second beer, which was the one with the low alcohol, and to be perfectly honest, even lower taste, I saw Sandy and Mandy walk in, and I was going to call out to them to come over, but remembered there were people here who like to act tough and everything, and that yelling would attract those people, and maybe Mandy and Sandy wouldn't even hear me above all the fucking noise anyway, so in the end I just waved, but they didn't see me.

They went to the bar, which I thought was pretty great because I didn't have to pay for everything for once, which I shouldn't really say, because Bruce had paid for the alcohol earlier, and I sat there drinking my beer, and after they'd bought their drinks they looked around some more and this time they saw me waving and came and sat down.

'Hi, I'm Mandy,' said Mandy.

'Hi, I'm Sandy,' said Sandy.

'Hello, I'm Wally,' I said. It was going tremendously so far, although at this point I'd run out of things to say, so I didn't say any other things.

'So,' said Mandy, looking at the empty glass in front of where Bruce wasn't sitting, on account of him not actually being here. 'Where's Bruce?'

'Oh, he's … well, actually, he's…' I knew it was wrong to lie. I knew Bruce was relying on me to bring these women home with me. I didn't understand why he even cared though. He was probably just thinking of me and my feelings, not wanting me to find his crushed dead body alone. He was a kind man, right to the end, I'd be able to say.

'Helloooo?' said Sandy, waving her hand in front of my eyes. 'Is there anybody in there?'

'Couldn't come,' I accidentally said. 'Unexpectedly detained. Saving the whales or something. You know good old Bruce,' I said, while having a horrible vision of Marisa and Larissa's blowholes.

'Oh, what a pity,' said Sandy.

'Will he be along later?' asked Mandy.

'Possibly,' I replied. 'Or we could just go and see him at home. I'm sure he wouldn't mind. Would anyone like a drink?'

'We already have drinks, thanks anyway Wally. Are you trying to get us drunk, take us home, tie us up and have your way with us?' asked Sandy, running her forefinger around the rim of her glass and looking up at me with her enormous blue eyes.

'Well, I…'

'Because if you are,' said Mandy, 'I think I just need to go to the toilet first, if that's alright?'

'Umm … Okay.'

'Back in a minute, Sexy,' said Sandy, dipping her forefinger into her glass and running it around my lips this time.

They giggled a lot as they wandered off to the toilets together. They were gone a really long time. Well, maybe it just seemed really long because at first I was very pleased indeed that Bruce was going to be very pleased indeed that I hadn't fucked it up and had got them to come back to my place. But then when they didn't come straight back from the toilets I began to wonder if maybe they were just toying with me, and weren't interested, so had just made fun of me and left.

Then I wondered if maybe they'd just gone to find some other guys there, some of the loudmouthed pub types who were making a lot of noise, and who would soon be here to beat me up and steal my wallet and leave me lying on the floor in a pool of my own blood and teeth on a patch of somebody else's vomit.

And then I wondered if maybe I was worrying too much about all this, because although men go to the toilet one at a time, and if one doesn't come back within a couple of minutes everyone knows he's in there doing a gigantic big shit, women are completely different to that. Women go to the toilet in groups, or at the least in pairs, and never come back very soon anyway, and obviously there's something going on in there that men have no understanding of, some secret women's business, and in fact now that I really thought about it I realised it probably had a lot to do with the toilet paper mystery, so Sandy and Mandy may just have been doing whatever the fuck it is that women normally do, which is almost certainly related to toilet paper, and would be back any minute.

'Hellooo? Is there anybody in there?' Sandy was saying as she waved her hand in front of my eyes again.

'You're cute Wally, but you're not the sharpest knife in the drawer are you?' said Mandy.

'Just how you like them,' said Sandy, and they both laughed like it was the funniest thing they'd ever heard.

We walked out to the car. We had a quick discussion where we decided what we'd do.

Sandy said, 'Mandy will go with you in your car, and I'll follow in mine.'

Like I said, it was a quick discussion. I was used to that. Masey and I used to have these sorts of discussions all the time. Well, she called them discussions anyway.

I didn't speak to Mandy at any time during the journey to my house, and she didn't speak to me either. She was on the phone. To Sandy. They were talking about chakras, and the moon, and how long the waiting list had become to get to see Doctor Hung.

38

And When I Say Harpoon…

WE ARRIVED at my house. Bruce's ute was still there. I hoped he'd somehow survived, but I didn't like his chances. We went inside. Barry White was doing his thing, loud and clear through the speakers, outside as well as in the lounge room.

'Wow, classy place. So where's Bruce?' asked Sandy. 'I'm really looking forward to meeting him. How long has he been an airline pilot anyway?'

'Yes,' said Mandy, 'did he become a pilot before you both joined the secret service or after, I'm a little confused.'

'Well, we're all a little confused,' I said. 'Would you like a drink ladies? There's a lot of really fabulous alcohol on the table over there. Pour some drinks and make yourselves comfortable. I'll just go and find him shall I?' I was being quite the host. I very much wished Bruce was still alive to see it. Just like he'd taught me.

Woof!

I went to the back door and cocked an ear — glad I didn't get that phrase mixed up — you could've heard a pin drop out there. Not that anyone dropped one. A pin I mean. I mean, they might have, but as I didn't hear one, I, well, I … Forget it … I walked over to the pool, expecting to see the somewhat chewed remains of Bruce floating face down in the water. The pool was empty. Except for the water. I walked back inside, just in time to hear Bruce laughing uproariously from upstairs.

I tried to get there first, but I was too late. Sandy led the charge, followed closely by Mandy, then myself.

'Holy shit,' said Sandy, Mandy, Bruce, Marisa and Larissa. They were all looking at each other, and nobody was looking at me. I was looking at all of them a little bit, and some of them a lot. I was trying really hard not to look at two of them in particular, but unfortunately for my poor eyes and brain, that task was beyond me.

There are moments in a man's life, Bruce would explain to me later, when he achieves something he could never have imagined, let alone dared to dream, or have others dream for him, or, umm, be paid by others to dream. Or something like that. When he was trying to explain it to me, I was still trying to block out the memory of what I'd seen on this night, so I wasn't really listening.

Sandy's mouth was open. Mandy's mouth was looking a lot like Sandy's mouth, although I noticed, just in a fleeting moment of awareness in the middle of all that was happening, that Mandy's mouth was quite large, and her tongue quite red, and her lips quite full, and

I briefly thought of my night with Tania. The thought didn't linger, overtaken as it was by the sight of Bruce trying with all his strength to push down the foot of my bed while wearing only my leather underpants on his head, as Larissa and Marisa, each wearing only a red climbing harness, hung like a pair of enormous white blimps above the bed at each end of a purple climbing rope, colliding every now and then with a wet slapping sound — two huge sweating mounds of blubber awaiting Bruce's tiny and completely inadequate harpoon. And when I say harpoon...

'G'day ladies,' said Bruce to Sandy and Mandy. 'Glad you could make it. Be with you in just a moment. Give us a hand Wally mate. Can't seem to get the girls down quite as far as the bed. Must have the belay device rigged up wrong. And they seem to weigh exactly the same as each other.'

'It's the way you've rigged it up to the bed here,' said Sandy.

'Sandy's a mountain climber,' said Mandy.

'Bewdy. I love mountain women,' said Bruce.

'What are these sluts doing here?' asked Marisa or Larissa. I still couldn't tell them apart, but they both seemed to have gotten fatter since I last saw them. I was just hoping they didn't burst over my bed. Even though I'd been unable to sleep in here since Masey left, it still held some fond memories. I can't remember them, but there must be some. Maybe Masey has them in Bali or Thailand or wherever the fuck she is.

'Who are you calling sluts?' enquired Sandy. 'You're the pair of fat bitches hanging naked from the rafters.'

Maybe she shouldn't have mentioned they were fat, but you had to admire her honesty.

'Get me down!' screeched Larissa or Marisa.

'Let's kill the slut,' screeched Marisa or Larissa.

I didn't care for their screeching, but didn't think it was a good time to upset them by saying anything.

'Well,' said Mandy, 'the fat bitches do have a point. We do fuck a lot of different men. Sluts is a bit strong though.'

'Yes, I suppose we do,' said Sandy. 'Actually, what's to stop us just fucking these two right now and leaving this pair of pork dumplings hanging in space watching.'

'Hahahahaahahahha, pork fucking dumplings,' Mandy shouted, loud enough for the neighbours to hear, and then she put on The Voice, the voiceover voice, and, well, nothing against fat people, but it was actually pretty fucking funny … 'PIGS IN SPAAAAAAACE.'

'You don't have to be mean,' said Marisa or Larissa. 'We can't help being big-boned.'

'Yes,' said Larissa or Marisa. 'And besides, Bruce certainly seems to like the way we're built, don't you Bruce?'

He'd been very quiet since the commotion had started.

We all waited to hear what he'd say. For some reason, it seemed like a lot was riding on it.

'Well,' he said, in a very clear voice…

And the doorbell went ding dong ding dong…

39

Show Us Your Truncheon, Officer

BRUCE SAID, 'We'd better get that Wally, it might be important. Stay here ladies, and don't make any noise. All of our lives may depend on it.'

He strode from the room with as much purpose as a naked man can muster, and I followed him down the stairs a bit before saying, 'Clothes Bruce?'

'Oh yeah,' he said. 'Still outside. I'll get them while you see who's at the door. Probably your neighbour complaining again. Fucker reckons we tried to drown his dog. Tell him to fuck off.'

All this time, the doorbell had continued to go ding dong ding dong... ding dong ding dong. Etcetera. I didn't want to answer the door, but I also didn't want the door to keep going ding dong ding dong all night. Someone might get cranky and call the police.

I opened the door. It was the police. I'd have recognised them anywhere. They hadn't got any bigger.

'Wallace Head,' said Lady Policeman. 'We'd like a word if you don't mind.'

'No problem,' I said. 'Which one would you like?'

Tiny Policeman looked at me in a menacing fashion and wrote something in his notebook. Then Lady Policeman pushed me aside and walked into my house, and Tiny Policeman followed her.

'Why don't you come in?' I said.

'Why don't you shut the fuck up and speak when you're spoken to?' said Lady Policeman.

'Right,' I said. 'I'll just shut up then, shall I?'

Tiny Policeman took out his truncheon, and I prepared myself to be beaten viciously about the head by closing my eyes very tightly and standing very still and waiting, but in the end, he didn't hit me at all. Nobody was saying anything, so I opened my eyes to see the Very Small Police Force looking at Bruce, who had stopped at the other side of the room to look at the Very Small Police Force. He was wearing my leather underpants and a rather becoming deerstalker cap. Fuck knows where he got it.

'Aha,' said Tiny Policeman. 'I see what's going on here. No wonder your wife left you. Sickos.'

'We've had a complaint Mister Head,' said Lady Policeman. 'An attempt on a neighbour's dog's life, apparently. Neighbour says he was roughed up and had his hat stolen too. Would you like to explain that for me?'

'I...I... Bruce?'

'Hello Officers. Perhaps I can explain. Wally here was out earlier, and I was having a bit of a swim in the pool with some guests, and there was a bit of splashing going on, and apparently the dog next door got wet. The lovely fellow from next door came over and we had a friendly chat and he left. Left his hat here too. Champion fellow. Bit confused though. Had a bit of a yell at me before he left and threatened to sick his dog onto me. Bit of the Old-timer's disease if you ask me. That's all. Everything's fine though. I won't be pressing any charges. And I must say, you both cut a fine figure in those uniforms. Very attractive indeed. I wish I could have served in the force myself, admirable thing it is, but when I applied they said I was too tall.'

'Right,' said Lady Policeman, 'so you're just a couple of gayboys having a little party then. Guests still here are they?'

'Oh no Officer. Decided to leave. Tickets to the ballet I think they said. Is it important?'

'I'm not gay!' I said.

'Shoosh Wally,' said Bruce. 'No Officers, it was a couple of lovely young ladies in fact. We're certainly not gay, and, well ma'am, if your male officer friend here doesn't mind of course, I'd be only too pleased to prove that to you by taking you out somewhere nice on a date. How's tomorrow night for you?'

Lady Policeman said, 'Well, I…'

Tiny Policeman said, 'Shall I hit him?'

Lady Policeman said, 'Officer Large! Where are your manners? Sorry about him, he's a bit careless with his truncheon.'

And Bruce said, 'Well we've all us men been guilty of that at times in our life, haven't we?'

I rubbed my forehead and tried to stay very still, and Lady Policeman was sort of smiling at Bruce and looking at his leather underpants, and then I became aware of strange sounds coming from upstairs, and Tiny Policeman was rubbing his truncheon in that weird way of his and saying, 'What's that noise upstairs?'

And Bruce said, 'Nothing at all Officer, you must be imagining it,' but it was getting louder, and quite frankly, even though Bruce is usually pretty good at saying just the right thing it was a really stupid thing to say, and nobody believed him.

So Lady Policeman said, 'Just be ready to use your truncheon, Large,' and they started to creep up the stairs.

And Bruce looked at Tiny Policeman and said, 'Large? Really?'

And Tiny Policeman whispered, 'You'll keep arse-hole. And shut the fuck up.'

Then they crept up the stairs some more, really very slowly, and we followed them, really very quietly.

I hoped the noises would stop; that the Tiny Police Force would just go away; that I'd wake up and think

Wow, what a shit dream — but they didn't; and they didn't; and I didn't.

And soon enough, or too soon, depending on your perspective, the Tiny Police Force sneaked all the way to the open door of what used to be my marital bedroom, and Bruce and I looked over their shoulders. There was Larissa or Marisa still hanging above the bed on one end of the purple rope while Mandy stood on the bed trying to wrap her lovely large mouth around as much of a gigantic bouncing bazoomba as she possibly could. Right next to them Marisa or Larissa hung from the other end of the purple rope doing her best not to scream with pleasure — or perhaps it was pain — as Sandy did a rather impressive job of attacking her Map-of-Tasmania with a darting, diving and definitely dextrous tongue.

I wanted to run, I really did, but the train wreck that was my life had just kept getting bigger, and it was unfortunately much too fascinating to do anything but watch.

Larissa or Marisa was the first to notice us in the doorway. 'Holy shit,' she yelled. 'Strippers! You guys sure do know how to party. This is fucking awesome.'

'Oh lovely, a man in uniform,' said Sandy. 'Show us your truncheon Officer.' In three seconds she had Tiny Policeman's pants down and was working as furiously on his teensy cocktail frankfurt with her mouth as it seemed possible to do without breaking the little thing off.

Tiny Policeman licked his lips lustfully and looked at Lady Policeman. Lady Policeman looked, not at Tiny Policeman, but at the vacillating vacuous vagina of the vainglorious vamp in front of her, shrugged her shoulders and went for it. Bruce tore off Lady Policeman's trousers and started humping away at her like a deprived dog on the world's most attractive leg. I stood there trying not to watch ... trying not to watch ... trying not to watch ... and wondered how I was going to explain all of this to Tess on Thursday. It seemed to me I'd find it impossible to explain this moment, so I took my phone out of my pocket and filmed a couple of minutes of it instead.

Then I went outside, thinking I might have a swim in the pool; decided against it when I considered what might possibly have happened to the water quality earlier in the evening; stood in the outdoor shower under what I hoped would be soul-cleansing streams of lukewarm water until my skin began to prune; and finally locked myself in the cabana to sleep the sleep that only a sane person in a world of mad persons can sleep.

40
Shapes of Sane

'OPEN UP WALLY,' Bruce was calling. 'C'mon mate, wakey wakey, hands off snakey. Got some brekkie for you.'

'Where am I,' I thought I thought. 'On the lounge,' I thought I thought. 'In the cabana,' I either thought or thought I thought. I couldn't be sure. A sleepy man with psychological and emotional troubles is an unreliable witness at best. I wrapped the sheet around me, crawled off the lounge, and unlocked the door.

'Big night you missed Wally. Here, get this coffee and brekkie into you,' said Bruce, handing me a steaming cup and a huge plate of extra-greasy bacon and sausages and eggs.

'Anyone else still here?' I asked.

'Fucken dead bodies everywhere mate. They're all here. Coppers had to leave after not long, but they both came back when they finished their shift and got the whole show on the road again. And those sick bitches you brought back from the pub are still here, and so's the fatties. Well done getting em back here too mate. Done yourself proud. My poor tadger'll never be the same again though. What the fuck happened to you anyway? Stage fright or what mate? Are you okay?'

'I don't really know Bruce. Just couldn't cope I guess. I just couldn't do it.'

'No shame in it mate. Lot of action for anyone. Maybe it was too quick to throw you in the deep end like that.'

'Why do you do it Bruce? It's all crazy. Maybe it's me, I don't know. It just doesn't seem right.'

'Dunno mate,' he said. 'Not for everyone I reckon. But me, I dunno … Maybe when my missus left it broke something in me. Maybe it was already broken. Losing my mum and dad, I dunno. Reckon you never get over that … But when there's a hole in your life, you fill it. Maybe that's all I've got. Maybe you're different though. She won't come back you know Wally. Your missus I mean … So, maybe you fill some holes by filling some holes. Sorry mate, that's all I can tell you.'

'But we're all crazy. We're all fucking nuts Bruce. Those young girls being so mean to people, putting everyone down all week, and then fucking you like maniacs on the weekend, why? Just because they're fat? They're beautiful young girls, they should be happy. And Rosemary and Tania and Sandy and Mandy, with all their plastic boobs and facelifts and all this talk of ropes and leather and dog collars, all trying to act young and hip, all fucking men they don't even know or care about. And that tiny policeman, hitting me with that truncheon thing every time I look at him, and the police girl, what's with her? I don't get any of it Bruce. And my son, he just ups and leaves the country and doesn't come back, why? No reason, just to see the world he says, bullshit it's bullshit I miss him he's my son and he never even calls me. And Masey. She brings home strangers and expects me to wife-swap or have group sex or I don't know what, it's all madness Bruce. Then there's you — Ha, you — your wife leaves and you think you can fuck your way to happiness, well you're as mad as any of them, and me? I must be the worst, I can't even hang around for the sex party. I film you all hard at it and slink away like a coward, I'm the worst of all I am. What's wrong with us Bruce? Are we all completely bonkers?'

'Maybe we're not Wally. Maybe that's just it, maybe we're the sane ones. What if there's more than one way to stay sane, and what if we're all just doing the best we can to be that. At least we're not just sinking under the weight of all the shit that's gone down. Yeah, maybe that mate. Just like the way we're all different sizes and shapes, right? And maybe that's the thing, maybe sanity has shapes, like people has shapes … Yeah … We're all hanging in there, all still sane, but we have to work at it. We're just different shapes of sane.' Then he counted on his fingers, as faster and faster he spoke. 'You and me, and your missus and kid, and the twins in there and the coppers and Sandy and Mandy. And them others too, that Rosemary and Tania and that Tracey you're friends with…'

'Tess.'

'Yeah, fucken Tess. And those two root-rats your missus pissed off to Thailand with. What's that, fifteen of us? Fifteen real people Wally, every one of us been through some shit or other you can bet your balls, and every one of us coping with however it shaped us by trying to reshape ourselves. Shapes of sane Wally. Fifteen shapes of sane. All of us, all in this together, every one of us doing the best we can, all tryin our best to help each other as well as ourselves … Waddaya reckon mate?'

'I reckon I need to think awhile Bruce.'

'Want me to get everyone out? I'll wake em all up and tell em to fuck off. I'll have to watch that little copper bloke though. Bit of small man about him. Seems to have taken a shine to the fat sheilas too. Threatened to run me in if I touched either of em again y'know. Didn't matter, I was done there anyway. Plenty of other dishes to sample.'

'Don't really like it much here Bruce. Might get away for a couple of days. You can stay. Enjoy your party. I just need to go somewhere and think awhile.'

'Know how you feel mate. Used to love my place, but I can't stand it now. Too quiet. Hey, why don't you go there? Nothing but solitude there. I'd get you the keys, but there's no locks on the place anyway.'

'Perfect Bruce. Thanks mate. You're a good friend.'

'No worries Wally. You're not bad yourself mate. Naaa, strike that, yer a fucken beauty. Best mate I ever had. Now get outta here before we turn into a pair of gayboys or somethin.'

'I'll meet you here Tuesday morning for work then?'

'No worries Wally. There's plenty of food in the fridge at mine. You might wanna take your own toothbrush though. Don't worry about this place. I'll look after it.'

I finished my breakfast and got out of there as quickly as I could. The last thing I wanted was to see any of our guests. It was nice, driving out to Bruce's mud brick house, down that long dead end street, all the way to the end, its only street frontage the driveway.

I sat on the dunny on that deck, looked out over the valley, and I shit and I shit and I shit. It was like I was purging myself of everything I'd ever held inside me, and when I was done I stepped off the deck and lay down in the dirt and I cried until I ran out of tears, with no-one to hear me but birds. And I listened to the birds, the screech-ing cockatoos and the magpies and the bellbirds and the laughing kookaburras, and I tried not to think — but I thought of Tess, and I heard her saying, 'So who are you now Wally?'

And I thought about it awhile, and I called Tess's number and asked her to come over even though it wasn't a Thursday, and she asked if I was okay, and I told her I was, and she said she'd be here in an hour.

41
A Shiny Diamond

I WAS ASLEEP in a big old armchair on the deck when Tess arrived.

'Okay Wally,' she was saying. 'What's happened? Are you alright?'

She looked beautiful. She was squinting against the sun, sending the little wrinkles running from her eyes. The sun was shining on her, lighting up the silvers of her hair, and my thoughts ran some weird line; Cleopatra, some old movie, memories of something you could never quite see or touch, some childlike happiness, the only sort of treasure worth keeping... I didn't tell her. I just smiled. She looked right into me, it made me happy, and I started to cry again.

'Oh Wally,' she said as she held my hand. 'It's alright. You're okay Wally. No need to talk, just let it all out.'

I didn't even know why I was crying. I was happy. Happier than I knew how to be, maybe that was the problem. I was here in this wonderful place because the man who owned it cared enough about me to let me be here. And there was someone visiting me because she cared enough to be here for me too. It wasn't as if nothing else mattered. It did. It was sad about Masey becoming so unhappy she'd had to leave me. And it was sad that James had gone to New York to get away from me, and maybe to get away from Masey too, and that made me sad for them both. And I was sad for myself too, but not for the me that's me now—only for all the lost years where I hadn't been myself, and had no clue who I was. And here I was, in this moment, standing on the threshold of a brilliant new life, and for the first time I could remember, I felt awake and alive and like a shiny fucking diamond made of skin and bone and flesh and mud and stone and luck and love, and some other wild thing that felt a lot like truth.

And all these things, I told Tess about them, and she sat and she listened and she looked at me like maybe I really mattered, and just when I felt the most natural yet electric yet scary yet perfect thing drawing us together, just when I felt I absolutely must kiss her, and if I didn't I'd die, she said, 'That's amazing Wally. What brought all this on?'

And I reckon, maybe, when she asked me, she saw in my eyes where my thoughts went, which was to all those fuckers, and when I say fuckers it isn't an insult, I only mean fuckers as in people who fuck—so yeah, all those fuckers at my house all fucking their way through the sad bits of their lives, and I reckon Tess saw a wrong look in my eyes, mistook what she saw for something else, and whatever spell we'd been weaving was broken, and she said, 'Let's have a cup of tea while you tell me some more.'

So I made the tea, and I told her what I could, and she kept her distance in every way you can think of. And yes, when I struggled to explain who was where, and how and why, the whole train wreck, when all those poor weird fuckers were starting their fuckings, I showed her the film I'd taken on my phone.

She watched in silence, but she watched. All the way to the end. And she said, 'Wallace Head. Do you honestly expect me to believe you weren't involved in this? What a wonderful actor you are. You and your silly friends and your amateur hour games. Ha! Thought I'd fall for your tears, your big sensitive act, let you do whatever sick depraved stuff you have planned for me too. Oh Wally. I really thought you were different. Purple ropes indeed. What the hell was I thinking?'

And she left without drinking her tea.

I asked her to stay, tried to get her to listen, to make her understand that I knew what she'd meant now, all that stuff about how I needed to find me, Wally, the real person I am, and that I'd done that.

But she walked, and she drove, and was gone.

42
How Zen of Me

A LOT had happened. I could have chased her, but that's what Wallace Head would have done. Crawled. Apologised. And people-pleased. Old Wallace Head would have done anything to appease the anger of the woman he'd married, or the company boss, or the young girl he'd accidentally insulted as she sat behind the reception desk at the medical centre. But I was no longer Wallace. I'd become Wally. So I sat, and I thought.

What would Wally do?

Wally would realise that Bruce had something there, that thing about the shapes. Tess had her own shit to deal with. Tess was lovely, wonderful, beautiful. What Tess was not, was perfect. She was her own shape of sane, and she would work this out for herself, and I would have to leave her alone so she could do just that.

How Zen of me, I thought. Or maybe just thought I thought. But there was no-one but birds here to tell me I was thinking out loud, and you know what, I said out loud for the birds to hear, the birds don't care what I think, or whether I talk to myself, or to them, or to nobody.

'I am Wally's shape of sane,' I said, good and loud, and a kookaburra laughed at me.

Then I picked up my phone and called James, because I missed him.

The phone didn't do anything for a while, because sometimes that's what phones do when you're calling someone who's on the other side of the world. And then, just when I thought it wasn't going to work, which is the only time it does start to work, it went brrt brrt, brrt brrt, brrt brrt, brrt brrt, and my little boy, my darling baby boy, in his big deep grown-up voice, said, 'Hi Dad, what's up?' and I wished I was there so I could have kissed him.

'Hi Son,' I said. 'It's been a while, and I know I'm a shit father, but I just wanted to hear your voice, and I wanted to tell you how much I miss you. Sorry.'

'Sorry for what Dad? Is everything alright? Nothing's happened has it? Is Mum okay?'

'She's fine James. Everything's fine. She's in Thailand you know. Having a holiday with some friends. Thailand.'

'Okay,' he said. 'So, how about you Dad? Why aren't you there too? And why do you sound so weird? Truth Dad. You never could tell a lie, not to save your life. Remember when I broke the stained glass window and you told Mum it was you? And she saw my cricket ball in amongst the broken glass, and you told her you'd been trying to put your shoes on, but the ball was in one, and it flicked through the window. And she pointed out that the ball should be outside then, and you said it bounced off a bird that was flying past and came back in, and that the bloody birds flying round were a menace. Bloody funny that was. And you still copped the shit for it, even though she knew it was me. So what's going on, tell me.'

'Nothing to worry about James, honest. I'm a shit husband and father, you know that. Your mum's had enough I guess. She's left mate. I don't think she'll come back. Are you okay?'

'Me? I'm fine Dad, what about you? How are you coping? It was always going to happen. You know how she is. Nothing's ever enough. You were always so different. Are you alright Dad? Do you want me to fly home? I'll come home if you need me. I can be there in three days. Just say the word.'

'Really James? You'd do that for me?'

'Of course. You're my dad. I'll book a flight as soon as I can.'

'James, son. I would so love to see you, I really would. But I'd be lying if I told you I'm not okay, or that I need you here now. I'm getting on fine. She's been gone a few weeks, and I've changed a bit—maybe even a lot. I miss you James, but you stay there and live your life mate. I'm finally starting to really live mine. Chucked my horrible job in and all. I'm mowing lawns now. And I love it!'

'Wow,' he said. 'Is this some mid-life crisis thing? Some sort of episode? Maybe I should come home and check on you.'

'No James, I'm fine, really I am. I worry about you over there alone, but I'm fine. Just finding out who I am. Anyway, I'm sure you're busy. Don't wanna waste your night talking to your old dad. It's night-time there now, right?'

'Yes Dad. I'm just out at a restaurant. I'll get going, but I really need to talk to you soon. On Skype, yeah? I want to see how you look. How about Monday? Monday night your time? Let's see, 7am here is 11pm your time, is that too late?'

'No, that's fine.'

'Great Dad. Skype you then.'

'Thanks son. And James ... I ... I mean, it's not easy for a dad, to say I mean, you know, but ... Well, I love you son.'

'I know Dad. Same. Monday night okay? Bye Dad.'

'Bye Son,' I said. And the phone went beep beep beep beep ... Actually, it didn't matter how the phone went. I was an old dog who'd learnt new tricks, and I had birds to listen to.

Woof!

43
Big Head v Small Head

I HUNG about Bruce's house, and I soaked up the silence, and the natural sounds that weren't silence but were in some way a kind of silence. And I went for walks, and dared to think thoughts of what my life could be, and felt really quite very alive.

On Monday night I drove back to my house about seven, as my computer was there and James would be calling at eleven. I thought maybe Bruce and I could have dinner together. If he wasn't otherwise engaged. Judging by the two extra cars in the driveway, it seemed that he was.

I let myself in quietly, thinking I'd just get something to eat and go out to the cabana until later, but Bruce had heard me arrive.

'Wally mate, how'd you go, feeling better?' he asked me.

'Yes Bruce,' I said. 'Couldn't be better. Sorry I'm early, my son's calling on Skype tonight so I had to come home.'

Home. It seemed the wrong word. Back. Back was more like it. Like in the past. I'd come Back.

Bruce had been talking, but I'd not heard a word.

'Sorry Bruce, what was that you said?'

'I said I've got my hands full upstairs mate, and I don't suppose you'd be up for helping a man out. Sandy and Mandy and Rosemary and that Tania chick that nearly fucked you to death. Knows her way around a cock that one don't she? They're all upstairs. Rosemary and Tania won't stop talking about that huge walloper of yours. Talk about making a bloke feel inadequate…'

I noticed Bruce's feelings of inadequacy weren't strong enough that he felt a need to wear any sort of clothing in front of me. Naked as the day he was born. Quite a bit hairier though, I'm willing to bet.

'Might pass mate,' I said. 'Should I take the computer out to the cabana? James is calling at eleven.'

'No way mate, it's your house. I'll tell em all to piss off home by ten. Leftover pad Thai in the fridge mate, saved it for you. I'd best get back to the action.'

I microwaved the food and Bruce went back to discovering new ways of shaping his sanity, interweaving it with that of others—and while to me it would always seem a sad impersonal thing, I also now saw that it made him happy. And I reckoned whatever made people happy and got them through life in one piece was okay by me, as long as they didn't drag anyone else into it.

Tolerant as well as Zen, I thought. I was like some kind of philosophical genius. With free microwaved Thai food.

It doesn't get much better than that. Instead of heading out to the cabana, I ate my food inside the house, put on some quiet Bach, then fell asleep on the rug in the lounge room.

I awoke to a face-full of female genitalia, and the feeling of a somehow familiar tongue and lips all over Young Wallace. I pushed the quite bald genitalia aside so I could see what was happening, and saw that it was attached to Rosemary, who was yelling 'Ride-im-cowboy,' and seemed to be rather desperate to ride my face no matter how rough the ride became.

Tania was doing her usual more than efficient job of arousing Young Wallace, who seemed to be conspiring against me. As much as my brain tried to put a stop to these shenanigans, Young Wallace searched happily for Tania's throat, and it seemed he had control once more of, not just the blood supply, but the everything else supply too.

It is surely a battle fought by men since the dawn of time, and here it was, played out just as it has been so many times before, a battle for control between the brothers Head. Big Head, trying to assert clear and rational thinking, trying to overrule Small Head, who, with control of the blood supply, preventing said blood from reaching the brain, was winning in his bid to do the primal thing, no matter the cost to the rest of the brain and the body.

In this particular case, of course, it wasn't just Small Head winning out over Big Head, but Young Wallace Head winning out over Old Wallace Head. 'But I'm not Wallace,' I thought I thought, 'I'm Wally.'

'Ooh yeah, you're Wally alright,' screeched Rosemary. 'Give us a suck of that big cock Tania you greedy bitch. Fuck me with your face Wally.'

And that was it. I'd remembered who I was. I was Wally. I only loved one woman. I had a mind of my own. I could make my own choices. And I only chose one woman. Not even my slightly bigger than average willy-wacker, or wolly-wicker, or wonky-winker was going to make my choices for me. I bucked both ladies off, jumped to my feet, and tried to run away.

44
It'll Probably Send Us a Christmas Card

My pants had been around my ankles of course. The coffee table was completely broken this time, but there was less blood than usual. Perhaps I was just running out of blood. Bruce was yelling at the ladies to fuck off out of this house right now. And something about being disgusted with their behaviour. And something else about them killing the best friend he ever had. All these things he was saying seemed to be at different times, like I was having sleeps between them, but after a while I found myself sitting up, quite awake on the lounge, with a nice cup of tea, and listening to Bruce and Sandy and Mandy talking about how those other bitches were nice enough girls, but had taken things too far on this occasion, although it might be nice to invite them over again next week, although not while Wally's around, his big bushwhacker's just too much temptation for them.

'Feeling any better Wally mate?' Bruce asked me. 'How's your tea going?'

'I'm fine,' I said. 'What happened?'

'I've told you four times mate. You were trying to escape the salaciously sexy suck-sisters. They sneaked down here and attacked you after we nodded off. Lucky we heard you yelling. You're fine now mate. How many fingers?'

'Three of course.'

'Bewdy. You're fine. Bit worried before. You answered Lion the first time I asked, and Trains the second time. What time's your kid calling?'

'James. Eleven. Skype.'

'There you go. You're fine. You've got half an hour then. Sandy and Mandy here are gonna get going, and I'll stay and make sure you're okay. Can't have you blacking out here all by yourself and carking it. No wonder you don't wanna play sexy games with everyone Wally. You're fucken accident prone mate.'

'You can see why they'd lose control though, can't you?' said Sandy.

'No kidding,' said Mandy. 'Biggest fucking cock I ever saw in my life.'

'Big? Big? That's not a cock, it's an entity. Rosemary reckons she saw it listed on the electoral roll,' said Sandy. 'It'll probably send us a Christmas card.'

'Alright ladies, that's enough,' said Bruce. 'You'd better piss off home before you lose control as well. Wally here couldn't survive another accident.'

Then Sandy and Mandy pissed off home.

45

It Sounded Like You Said Jonathon

'Bruce,' I said. 'Do you think Sandy and Mandy might not have seen many men naked?'

He laughed. A lot. Really quite loudly. 'Good one Wally. What the fuck are you on about now?'

'Well I know it's fun to have a laugh about the size of people's willies and all, and I know I've had a hit on the head, but anyone would have thought they were serious just now. About my wee willie I mean…'

'Wally. Mate. Sandy and Mandy have had more dicks in em than you and me have had hot dinners. That heat-seeking missile of yours is a fucken monster. As if you didn't know. You better not be trying to get me to feel it…'

'No! No, Bruce, I just…'

'Well thank fuck for that. I'd never get my hands around the monstrous fucker. Dunno how you manage to control the bastard when you go for a piss. Must be like a fucken fire-hose. So what's with all the silly questions? Something wrong mate? Are you okay?'

'Yes. I mean … so it really is big then?'

'You're shitting me Wal. You never knew? Mate, I told you, the only place I ever saw a lump of meat like that was in a zoo or a farmyard. There'd be giraffes jealous of that thing. Did you really not know? Hardly seems possible mate. No-one ever told you? Or fucken screamed and ran away when they saw it? That'd be a clue.'

'I … Masey's the only person who's ever seen it until recently. She never said anything. I suppose she just thought it was average too. I'm sorry to get so personal with you Bruce. I just needed to know. Not sure why.'

'No worries Wally. You can hold your head high with that thing mate. Actually, you better hold your head high. That bastard could knock your head clean off if it went hard in a hurry. Anyway, you better get ready for your phone call mate. I'll go have a feed, then I'd better go wash some of this dirty sex off me. I must smell like a two dollar whore at the arse end of a twelve hour shift.'

Bruce wandered off to the kitchen, leaving me and my sore head to think about things again. But I didn't have long. James would be calling soon, so I turned on the computer and signed into Skype so I'd be all ready.

If only I'd known what I'd been getting all ready for, I might have been more, or less, ready. But I didn't, and I wasn't.

A minute after eleven, the computer went DooBooDo, DoBeDooDo, DooBooDo, DoBeDooDo.

Who doesn't love the Skype incoming call sound? Best music ever.

DooBooDo, DoBeDooDo.

I was looking forward to seeing and talking to James, but I decided to listen to just one more round, Doo-BooDo, DoBeDooDo.

And just one more, DooBooDo, DoBeDooDo.

Okay, two and that's it. DooBooDo, DoBeDooDo, DooBooDo, DoBeDooDo.

I clicked on the Accept Video Call button.

Nothing happened, then more nothing, then I said, 'Hello?'

Then I saw James, and he said, 'Hi Dad, just a minute. Nice beard,' then some other stuff happened, there was some clicking of buttons and people saying yes and no and hello this and are you there that, and I could hear the shower running, and I wondered if maybe I'd been hit harder on the head than I thought this time, then Masey was on the screen too saying, 'What's your father doing here?'

And I thought of saying "I could say the same," except I didn't because I wasn't quite sure if it was exactly the thing I wanted to say, and it felt really strange to be seeing Masey, and I wondered if maybe I was dreaming it, and then it was sort of too late to say it anyway, because we'd obviously moved on from there, and James was giving us both a bit of a lecture about it being fine to separate, divorce and whatever else we chose to do, but he was still our son and there was no reason not to get along when he had something important to tell us.

So I said, 'Of course James. You're right.'

And Masey said, 'Oh, stop interrupting Wallace. Not everything's about you, you know. And what is that ridiculous hairy growth all over your face?'

And I said, 'My name's not Wallace, it's Wally.'

And Masey said, 'Fine, I'll try to remember that for the divorce papers. Wallace.'

And James said, or rather yelled, 'Enough!'

'Yes, Dear,' said Masey. 'Your father will shut up now. What would you like to say? It's so lovely to hear your voice. You look a bit pale though. And what is that awful mess in my lounge room Wallace? Is that broken pile of wreckage my two thousand dollar coffee table? What have you been doing to my house you useless piece of shit?'

I looked behind me. It certainly was a broken pile of wreckage. You wouldn't think one head could do that much damage. I must have hit it with my body too.

'I thought it was my house too,' I said. It was the best I could think of under the circumstances.

'I'll cut your balls off you useless softcock. I'll…'

'Mum,' James shouted. 'Please listen. Please. For once in your life … Please.'

And there was quiet. It may have been the first time I'd ever heard Masey that quiet. I wondered if she'd been disconnected.

'Mum, Dad. I'm getting married.'

'Oh that's preposterous,' said Masey. 'When did you meet this girl? Ridiculous.'

'Mum!'

'Congratulations James,' I said. 'Well done. What's her name?'

'Jonathon,' I thought he said.

'Oh dear,' Masey said. 'This line's simply awful. Heehee. It sounded like you said Jonathon.'

'I did,' he said.

Clearly, I'd been hit harder on the head than I thought. The conversation seemed real enough, but the chances of James meeting and marrying a woman called Jonathon were, after all, not very likely.

I looked around. The wreckage of the coffee table matched the wreckage of my skull. It could be real. The pain was real. The shower was still running. I was here, so it must have been Bruce in the shower, and I knew he was real—I could still smell the food he'd heated up before he went into the shower.

'One of those dreadful arty types is she James darling? Going by a boy's name. Silly girl. We'll soon see about this. Is she from a good family? I simply won't give my permission if she's not. I can make things very difficult for you if I have to James. Well, what have you to say for yourself?'

'Mum, stop it. Jonathon's twenty-seven, we've been together two years, and we're very much in love. He asked me to marry him three nights ago, and I've said yes.'

'She asked you?' said Masey. 'Smacks of desperation if you ask me. What's the world coming to? I'm all for women's rights, but what a desperado. She's obviously got you quite brainwashed Darling.'

'Mum. Stop calling him a girl. And stop … everything. Can't you be happy for me? Please Mum. You've always known I was gay, surely. It's time to stop pretending. I'm a man now. A gay man. I'm very much in love, and Jonathon feels the same way. We've been in a monogamous relationship for two years, and we're going to spend our lives together. That's it. That's all. Enough Mum. Please.'

'Ludicrous,' said Masey. 'Gay. Of course you're not. Have you even tried dating girls? Don't knock it until you've tried it, that's my motto now. Unlike your useless prude of a father. Have you died Wallace? Do you have nothing to say to your ridiculous son about this? Wallace? Useless piece of shit.'

'Dad?' said James.

'So … you're … gay then?'

'Yes Dad. You didn't know?'

'Fucking idiot,' said Masey.

'Mum!'

'Okay,' I said. 'So, this Jonathon. Is he a … nice man?'

'Yes Dad, he's lovely.'

'And … I suppose … he's gay too then?'

'Yes Dad, Jonathon's gay too.'

'Well I suppose that should work out fine then son. Congratulations! When's the wedding?'

'You fucking softcock bastard,' said Masey. 'Is that all you have to say? Useless…'

'Mum, stop! I'll hang up on you and never speak to you again, seriously. Please. This should be a happy time. Please Mum. And thank you Dad. It means a lot to me.'

'Oh he's just sucking up to you James. He doesn't mean it.'

'Mum, stop. Right now. Dad's always been the tolerant one. You should be nicer to him. Really.'

'Ummm … James,' I said. 'Just wondering, if you're gay, and Jonathon's gay, then … I mean, who's who? Like, who's the boy and who's the girl? I mean … oh shit, sorry.'

'Oh, for fuck's sake,' said Masey.

James laughed. 'Dad. You don't really want me to explain that do you? I mean … really?'

'Your father's a moron James.'

'No … Oh, no no no.' I said. 'Oh shit! I just meant, like if you get married, and you're both men, then am

I the father of the groom or the bride? Do I pay for the wedding, and…' My head hurt.

'Hilarious Dad. We're both the groom. We're just men. We ride mountain bikes, play tennis, go rock climbing. And Jonathon plays ice hockey. You'll like him. We're just men Dad. You really are hilarious. What's that cut on your head?'

'Oh, I tripped on my pants and fell onto the coffee table earlier. I'm fine Son.'

'Yes, just look at what he's done to it,' said Masey. 'Probably destroyed the whole house while I've been gone. I paid a fortune for that table and now look at it.'

'Ummm, Dad. Who's that behind you, and why is he naked?'

I looked behind me. It was Bruce, who'd finished his shower and appeared to be searching for his pants.

'Oh my God Dad! No wonder you took it so well. You're gay too!' said James

'For fuck's sake,' said Masey. 'Is that Bruce? You're fucking the gardener? You sick bastard Wallace.'

'What are you talking about Mum? We can't see his face. Unless… Oh my goodness!'

I looked at Bruce. He looked at me. I thought… Well, I didn't think. It was… things were… James was gay and getting married. I wasn't gay, but Bruce was naked, and James and Masey had seen him. And Bruce wasn't gay.

Was he? No of course not. But…?

'I…I didn't say it was Bruce,' said Masey. 'I didn't say anything. It was your father.'

'He hasn't said a word Mum. You've BOTH been fucking the gardener! Unbelievable!'

'I never fucked anybody,' I said. 'Except Tania.'

'Who the fuck is Tania?' said Masey. 'That bitch better not be in my house.'

Bruce was still looking at me, and I was still looking at him. He had his hands covering his genitals now, and he looked like he wasn't too sure what to say. 'I'm sorry Wally,' he said. 'It was only a few times, and I never even knew you yet. I'm sorry mate.'

'Shut the fuck up you idiot,' screamed Masey. 'Oh God. Another moron. He'd never have known. Do stop dripping water all over my rug Bruce darling, you'll ruin it. How are you anyway Gorgeous? Fit as ever I see. Do get a towel will you? Seriously, that rug cost a fortune. I didn't know you were bi Bruce. You must meet my friends Derek and Cyn when I come home. I'll call you.'

And that was when I understood.

46
Would You Like Your Hedge Trimmed?

'MASEY. Please shut up,' I said. 'James. I'm not gay, Son. Bruce has been staying here. I thought we were friends. We double dated a few times. He was showing me the ropes.'

'Mmmm lovely, I didn't know you were into ropes Bruce darling.'

'Shut up Masey. You really should learn to let others speak sometimes. You can be such a bully. James, I'm so glad you're happy Son, and I look forward to meeting your wife. Husband. Jonathon. Your Jonathon. But I must go now, I have something to discuss with my former friend Bruce, who is a liar, and has, as you have seen, rather small genitals.'

'Hey, steady on Wally, they're actually above average. We can't all have a magic wand that has its own area code. And I'm sorry mate. I didn't even know you then. And she begged me mate. I...'

'Begged you?' screeched Masey. 'Fucking begged you? Desperate for it you were. Wandering past the windows with your shirt off, sweat dripping off you, flexing those muscles ... As I recall it, you asked me if I needed my hedge trimmed...'

'That's ridiculous. We don't even have a hedge,' I said.

'It's metaphorical Dad,' said James.

'Oh,' I said. 'Ohhhhh.'

'You silly fucker Wally,' said Bruce. 'That's hilarious mate. Don't worry, I'll show you tomorrow at work. Works a treat. Great way to start banging the customers.'

'Tomorrow at work?' said Masey. 'What the hell are you talking about?'

'Wally works for me now Mase. Mowing lawns. He's a natural.'

'That's it. Destroying my house, quitting your job, what the hell is wrong with you Wallace Head? How are we going to afford to live? You will march yourself back to your real place of employment and beg for your job back first thing tomorrow. And I will be seeing you as soon as I can get a flight back.'

'Masey,' I said. 'Do not bother. And please imagine the names I would now like to call you, but cannot because our son would hear. Consider yourself told all of these names, plus some others you cannot possibly imagine. Also, I will not be returning to my old job. Ever. I do not like you, and you are not the boss of me. And my fucking name is Wally. Is that so difficult to remember?'

'You fucken tell her Wally mate,' said Bruce.

'Bruce,' I said. 'Get out of my house right now. Do not come back. I do not work for you any more. You are a cheating slimy pathetic piece of slug-shit, and I will be immensely happy if I never see you again. Goodbye. And Bruce…'

'Yes Wal?'

'I hope your pathetic little sausage rots off.'

'Bit rugged that mate. I said I was sorry.'

He just didn't get it.

'James. I have to go Son. I love you very much, I'm very happy for you, and I hope your marriage will be based in love and truth and trust. I know this night hasn't gone exactly as you would have hoped, but sometimes the lessons we learn are what's important. And there's certainly some lessons to be learned here. I wish you and Jonathon every happiness, and a wonderful life together. Goodnight Son.'

'Love you Dad,' he said. I clicked on the End Call button, and the computer went Boooooorrup.

'Well that went well,' said Bruce.

'Are you still here?' I replied. 'Please be gone by the time I'm out of the shower.'

I walked to the shower, and even though many strange things had just happened, it no longer felt like a dream. I was Wally Head, and shit had gone down, and I had held my head high.

What was left of it.

47

A Shape Must Be Earned

I DREAMED of lions again. Hyenas too, and wildebeest and giant kangaroos and bald rats and a meerkat, and a train that wouldn't stop when people needed to get off. And a giraffe. The giraffe was looking around at stuff, but it couldn't see what it wanted to because its head was above the clouds. It was a pretty stupid dream.

I made myself some coffee and drank it. I cooked bacon and sausages and eggs and baked beans and tomato. Enough for two people, maybe more. I burnt the toast. It popped up without burning, but I put it back down and charred it on purpose. The smoke alarm went FUCKING BEEP BEEP BEEP BEEP BEEP BEEP BEEP BEEP BEEP BEEP BEEP BEEP BEEP BEEP BEEP BEEP until I broke it with a saucepan. I should have used a clean one instead of the one that still had the baked beans in it, but it was too late to be thinking about that after I'd done it.

I ate everything I'd cooked except for what beans were on the floor. I didn't eat them because there were bits of plastic from the smoke alarm all through them.

I didn't clean up the mess. I didn't pick up the broken bits of coffee table either.

Masey had said she was coming home. I really needed to show her how much I appreciated her. I took the painted portrait of her off the wall and put it in the middle of the lounge room floor—then I did a big shit right in the middle of it. I'm an artist, I thought. Bull shit artist, no bull. If I was famous, people would have paid money for that.

I drank more coffee, and thought about my life. James was gay. It was unexpected. But maybe it explained his need to get away from here. Maybe it hadn't been me or Masey at all, and we'd been looking at it all wrong. We weren't great parents, but who is? We'd both done our best. He was gay. He'd needed to break free, to find himself. Maybe to read fifty self-help books, live in New York, meet all new people who had no expectations of him. Shapes of sane. He'd found his shape, and he was happy. It was all that mattered.

And Masey, maybe she was happy too. She wasn't happy when she was with me, and she wasn't happy on the phone last night, but that was because I was there. She sure did spark up when she saw Bruce though. Bits of Bruce. It still hurt. But she was different, she'd moved on, and I had too, in my way. She knew what she wanted. Didn't we all? But what we wanted wasn't usually what we could have. That was never really the way this worked. You can't be the shape you wanna be just because you want it. A shape has to be earned, whether it's the shape of a body, a shape of sanity, or a shape of happiness. There was plenty to what Bruce had said. Maybe he was wiser than either of us knew.

Bruce. All along, acting like the best friend a bloke could ever have. All the fun and conversation, the good advice and the laughter. All the care and the friendship, the help freely given to move on, to get through a really difficult time in my life, and become the best person I could be. While all along, he knew just how it felt to have my wife under him, or over him, or...

Fuck him. She did.

Fuck him.

He'd be at work now. I'd have been there with him, and he'd have been trying to teach me how to get the customers into bed. But not telling me how he'd done it with Masey.

Fuck them both. With a barbed and rusted fishing spear. Preferably fired from a very powerful speargun. One which hasn't been cleaned since it was used to spear several now rancid fish some days ago.

Everyone should have what they deserve, I reckon. Thing is though, sometimes they don't know what that is, so other people have to intervene, and bring it to them.

It was my turn to make that stuff happen. I picked up the phone, called the bank and my solicitor's office, and made all the arrangements.

48
Purple-Headed Junket-Pumper

MASEY ARRIVED in a taxi early Thursday morning. Silver Service. Couldn't have an ordinary taxi pulling up in our driveway. She was somebody. Just ask her. She'll tell you. Just another way to spend money if you ask me. But you can't make a silk person like a sour ear. Or whatever they call it.

She made the poor guy carry all her bags in. Six bags. I lay on the lounge where I'd slept, and didn't offer to help. She paid him and he looked really grateful. Whether she tipped him well or did him a favour in the taxi on the way I'll never know. And I didn't much care. I was more interested in getting some coffee without having to put up with too much of Masey's whinging.

'Hello Wallace Dear,' she said. 'Wonderful job you've done of the decorating. Smashing job, one might say.'

It was kind of funny, and I laughed even though I didn't want to. She'd been funny once, Masey. When we were young. Ha. Smashing job. Apart from the wreckage of the coffee table, I'd made a large pile of interestingly shaped canvas and broken frames on top of the shitted on portrait, having decided to improve the look of the place by putting my head through a few of the more horrible pieces of art, then piling them in the middle of the room. Probably for the best really. The magnificent shit I'd done on her professionally painted face probably wouldn't have gone down too well after all. Might have won a prize in the right art competition though. Truth be known, Masey had paid good money for worse art than a shit-covered face. At least it made a clear and honest statement.

'Don't just lie around all day Wallace, we have a home to put back in order. You can start by making us some coffee while I put my clothes away. I'm sure you can at least manage that. And not that rubbish instant stuff Dear, you know I can't stand it.'

She went upstairs, I went to the bathroom. She put away her clothes, I pissed in the toilet. She came downstairs while I was making the coffee.

'Wallace Dear,' she said.

'Yes Masey?' I prepared to be hit.

'Why does our bedroom appear to have been the venue for a National BDSM convention?'

'Bruce and I had a few friends over.' I closed my eyes and tried not to cringe, determined to take it like a man.

'Hmmm. Fab setup with the ropes and all. There may be hope for you yet Wallace. I don't suppose you thought to clean the kitchen while I was gone? Goodness me, what the hell is that? I hope you weren't eating it,' she said, examining the remains of the smoke alarm that had melted onto the bottom of the saucepan, which now hung from the *industrial retro avant-garde* light fitting.

'Well, a man needed a hobby. Best to just give the ladies what they want, Bruce always says. But you knew that already Masey, didn't you?'

'Well I am so terribly sorry Wallace, but what was I to do? Don't you start on me. You were always at work, then you'd come home and never even notice me. A woman has needs you know.'

'Well I'm sorry it didn't work out Masey. But at least you have your friends Derek and Cynthia don't you? And fuck knows who else. And stop calling me Wallace. My name is Wally. If you can't call me Wally, don't bother speaking to me. In fact, don't bother anyway.'

'Fine then,' she said in her poutiest voice. 'See if I care. But Wallace … Wally … Tell me about this Tania woman. Did you … enjoy her?'

I looked at her. She didn't look angry, only interested. What the hell, I thought, it doesn't matter anyway. 'Yes I did Masey. She licked my maraca sack all over, then sucked my purple-headed junket-pumper till she choked on the contents. Then she rode me until she was saddle-sore and it was fan-fucking-tastic. Any more questions?'

'Been subscribing to Word of the Day have we Dear? Where did you get all those ropes and harnesses and things?'

'Climbing gym. Anything else?'

'Well, Wallace … Wally … Do you think we could, maybe, invite Derek and Cyn over, and, you know … I mean, there's no reason we can't all get along now is there?' She moved in, closer, closer, her eyes trapping me. She knew exactly what she was doing. 'I'd forgotten what a sexy man you can be, and…'

'Right Masey. So you think you can sleep around with God only knows who, for fuck knows how long, and then because you see something about me you like again things can all just go back to normal? Fuck Masey, what's wrong with you?'

I broke away from her gaze and took my coffee outside to the cabana. She followed.

'I'm sorry Wallace. I'm sorry. We can work this out…'

I closed the cabana door. I wanted her to suffer awhile.

After an hour I knew I had her. She brought me breakfast. Who held the cards now? I should have done this years ago. Who knew? A bit of broken art and furniture, some rope and harnesses, a surly bad-boy attitude, and Wally Head was Master in his own home. For the first time ever, what I wanted mattered. It felt good, but I didn't let on.

'Anything else I can get you Dear?' she asked. 'More coffee perhaps? We really must look after you better. I'm so sorry Wally. But we can move on. We can have a wonderful life now.'

'Perhaps we can,' I said. 'A bit more sugar in the coffee next time Masey.'

'Yes Darling,' she said. 'Whatever you want.'

She tried to kiss me, but I held her off. 'Not yet Masey,' I said. 'Not yet.'

'Of course Dear,' she said. 'I understand. Things will be good again.'

'Yes,' I said. 'Things will. We're going to be so happy. Let's clean the house eh?' I smiled at her, and we went inside.

49
You Saved Me, Head

WE SPENT the next few hours cleaning up. It hadn't been too bad until a few days ago, apart from the kitchen of course. Well, I'd been angry. But I was over that. It was time to make things right. By four o'clock the house was in shape, and I'd managed to shield Masey from seeing that I'd shit on her face while I was angry. We were sitting down to a late lunch when the doorbell went ding dong ding dong... ding dong ding dong... ding dong ding dong... ding dong ding dong.

It was Thursday afternoon, and my heart went flitter with the dings, and flutter with the dongs, and part of me wished it was Tess, and part of me dreaded that it might be. Masey and I pretended not to race each other to the door, and pretended we didn't know or care who might be there.

It was the Tiny Police Force. Just when things were going so well. 'Wallace Head,' said Lady Policeman.

'Hello,' I said. 'Call me Wally.'

'What the hell have you been up to Wallace? Wally?' said Masey.

'Do I have the pleasure of addressing Mrs Head, ma'am?' enquired Lady Policeman.

'Yes, that is correct. I'm Masey Head. Can I help you?'

'No thank you ma'am. You're even prettier than your photo. We just need a minute of your husband's time. In private, if you don't mind.'

'Why thank you,' said Masey. 'I still have a little unpacking to do. Lovely to meet you.' She was obviously impressed. I couldn't tell whether she was impressed with the police wanting to speak to me or that someone thought she was prettier than her photo, but she looked awfully impressed about something. She looked at me strangely and went upstairs.

'Close the door please Masey,' I called out. She closed the door.

'Sexy woman,' said Lady Policeman.

'Could use a bit of feeding up if you ask me,' said Tiny Policeman.

'And to what do I owe this visit?' I asked as politely as I could manage. 'Truncheon practice perhaps?' I rubbed my head.

'You have some new ones on your forehead I see. Lovely work too,' said Tiny Policeman, obviously impressed.

They looked at each other, then Lady Policeman spoke. 'We've come to thank you, Mister Head. You'd better go first, Large.'

'Wally,' he said. 'Can I call you Wally? I want to thank you. If it wasn't for you, I'd just be a lonely police officer. But because of you, I'm the happiest man alive. Marisa, Larissa and I are moving in together. Life's too short to go through it sad and angry. Sure, there's a place for violence, and the truncheon's vital to good police work, and a wonderful hobby besides, but I've discovered there's more to life. I love those girls. The noses on them! Along with their other, ahem... attributes. Such lovely, beautiful girls. And you know, once you get to know them, they're really very nice people. They just needed someone to love them. By the way Head... If you ever speak to either of them again, I'm going to kill you. But thank you. And they said to thank you too. Oh, and Marisa gave me this printout of your blood test. Apparently your cock isn't going to rot off after all. So stay away from the Medical Centre, Wally. I mean it. And thanks again.'

'Ah, so Marisa's the one who works at the medical centre. Finally I know which one's which.'

'Actually you don't Wally, they swap around. Nobody knows which is which, not even me. Wouldn't have it any other way.'

'Then how'd you know it was Marisa who said to tell me that?'

'Because she said to tell you Larissa said it, and they're both complete liars.'

'Well, thank you Officer Large. I'm glad you're all happy, and I'll be only too happy to respect your wishes and never speak to any of you again.'

'You'd better Wally,' he said, rubbing his truncheon as only he can.

'Go get the gift Large. And take your time,' said Lady Policeman, and he walked out to their patrol car.

'I wanted a private moment,' she said. 'Firstly, does your wife swing both ways?'

'Ummm...I'm not completely sure, but I suppose you could ask her.'

'I will then. Mister Head, I was married when I was young. He was an officer too, and a bad man. Also, the sex was lousy. Second best day of my life was when he pissed off with another woman. Been alone for ten years since then, and never had sex in all that time. Then you came along.'

'Me? I didn't do anything! I was in the cabana. I...'

'Be quiet Head. Pull yourself together. I mean, that night, here...that filthy disgusting orgy you organised...I saw that beautiful pussy in front of me and everything just fell into place. Greatest moment of my entire life. It was like I had no control, like it was my destiny. I found myself licking that juicy snatch, and I didn't even care about your big depraved friend humping away at me. I just imagined he was a tall hot woman with short dark hair and a lovely big dildo. Does your wife have a good variety of dildos Head?'

'I, ummm, think she might have. You'd have to ask her.'

'Good. I'll ask her. Anyway, thanks Mister Head. I was going to go home and blow my head off at the end of my shift that night, but thanks to you, I found out just who I am. You saved me Head. Thank you. And put in a good word with your wife for me, would you? You're a good fella. For a straight guy.' She turned toward the street. 'Large! Bring the gift.'

Officer Large carried a big white box, wrapped with a huge red ribbon, up from the car and put it just inside the front door. 'Thank you Wally,' he said. 'And stay the fuck away from my women or you're dead meat.'

Then Lady Policeman shook my hand, said, 'I'll drop in Friday night to check the gift's okay. Say hi to your wife for me,' and they left.

50
Making Zombie Noises

I CLOSED the front door and looked at the box.

'What the hell have you been up to?' asked Masey as she came down the stairs. 'And what's in that box? There's more to you than I realised Wallace Head, and I think I like it.'

'Just some friends, Masey. Are you bisexual, by the way?'

'Of course Wally. Isn't everybody really? I do like your line of questioning, I must say. Can we invite Derek and Cynthia over? Please Wally?'

'Why not,' I said. 'Tell them to be here at eight-thirty and not a minute before. And to pick up some Thai food on the way. Some quality scotch too. We seem to be out. Now let's see what's in this box.'

I untied the red ribbon, and tried to open the box.

'You're doing it all wrong,' said Masey. 'Here, let me.' A lifetime of unwrapping things she'd wasted our money on came in handy, and the box was open in seconds.

It seemed to be some sort of survival kit. If you were trapped in a dungeon with only a few BDSM practitioners for company.

'Ooooooh,' said Masey. 'Aaaaaaaaah.' Clearly she liked the look of all this black rubber. Especially the mask. I put it on and pretended I was a zombie.

'Be serious,' she said.

I ignored her, continued to have fun making zombie noises, and left the mask on. The handcuffs were obviously a highlight for Masey, and there was a special moan of appreciation when she unearthed a large black dildo with its very own bright pink spinning finger. It made a particularly irksome whirring sound when she turned it on. If she'd asked me, I'd have told her it looked like Doctor Frankenstein had really fucked up this time. But she didn't ask, and I didn't tell.

What she did ask, was why. 'Why did the police bring you all these lovely toys?'

'New Police Force initiative. Get to know your local Constabulary. Bringing everyday police work into people's homes. It was in the local paper on Tuesday. By the way, did you fancy the lady officer? She certainly took a shine to you.'

'Well, she's kind of cute in a conventional way. She could do with a bit of work though. A good boob job and some Botox would do wonders for her.'

'Well, she's coming over this Friday night to get to know you better. Perhaps you can give her Doctor Hung's number. Be kind though. She's a bit fragile. Had a hard life, and it can't be easy being a lady copper.'

'Oh Wally. You're so lovely and considerate.'

The doorbell went ding dong, ding dong, and Masey opened the door.

The doorbell went ding dong, ding dong, and I noticed Masey still had the black and pink dildo in her hand. With its engine still running, its strange appendage seemed to be beckoning the person standing in the doorway to come closer.

The doorbell went ding dong, ding dong, and I noticed the person standing in the doorway was Tess.

The doorbell went ding dong, ding dong, and my poor little gigantic fucking heart went, not just flitter flutter, but KaFuckingBoomBaDoomBoom.

'Can I help you?' asked Masey.

'I'm sorry,' said Tess. 'I seem to have turned up at a rather inopportune moment. Nice mask Wally. Quite the improvement. Goodbye.' And she turned and started walking away.

'No, wait!' I said.

'Who is this person, Wallace?' asked Masey.

'She's ... she's ...' They were looking at me. Both of them. A lot. In that way only women can, and that makes you realise this moment is really important, but you have no idea why, or what you should do. 'She's Tess, that's who she is. She's...'

'I'm no-one important,' said Tess. Wally and I have been exercising together. A walk in the park on Thursdays, that's all. I should have called. Nice meeting you…'

'Masey Head. Wallace's long-suffering wife. So you're Tess are you? Funny, Wally never mentioned you.' She turned off the vibrator.

'Well, as I said, I'm not important,' said Tess. 'And please. Call me Therese. Well, it's time for my walk. I'll leave you to your… fun.' And she smiled one of those tiny tight smiles that isn't one, and walked away like I didn't matter.

I took off the stupid mask. Masey looked at me funny.

'Oh dear, Wallace,' she said, as Tess climbed into her car. 'Scraping the bottom of the barrel with that one weren't you? Goodness me. How positively ghastly. Did you see those grey hairs? And the wrinkles! I do hope none of the neighbours noticed. And her car! Wasn't that one of those awful Eco-cars? The electric ones? Ugly things. I've heard of people looking like their pets, perhaps it applies to their cars too.'

I stood and watched Tess drive away. 'You don't have to be mean,' I said. 'She's a very nice person.'

'Oh Wally. What good is nice? Poor meek thing, getting around with that flat chest and all those ghastly wrinkles around her eyes and mouth.'

'They're called laugh lines Masey, not wrinkles.'

'Oh, who told you that? The girl clearly has nothing to laugh about. Doesn't even have the self-respect to go and get herself a boob job. Ridiculous long-necked thing. Come inside Wallace. We really should shave that beard of yours off before Derek and Cyn arrive. You'll need it gone to go and get your job back next week anyway. I do love you Dear, but we have a certain lifestyle and standards we need to uphold.'

I stood in the doorway with the stupid rubber mask in my hand, then I put the mask back on and walked inside. But I didn't feel like making zombie noises.

51

Partners in Porn

MASEY BUSIED herself getting the house ready for Derek and Cynthia. It was really quite civilised. She even cleaned the ropes and harnesses, and washed the new dildo.

'You never know where one's been, not even a new one,' she said with a glint in her eye.

At eight o'clock Masey was showering, readying herself for the fun night ahead. On the bed she had laid out for me a complete new outfit, including a surprisingly shiny new pair of leather underpants. These had studs on them large enough to tear the mouth out of anything silly enough to attack them. It was a pleasant thought, but I didn't put them on. For some reason I hoped I wouldn't dream of next door's dog. I wore jeans and a T-shirt. No shoes. Went just right with Masey's low-cut, backless, and mostly sideless evening gown I thought.

The doorbell went ding dong ding dong... ding dong ding dong, and Masey said, 'Best behaviour tonight Wallace. I do wish you'd worn your lovely new suit.'

Then the doorbell went ding dong ding dong... ding dong ding dong, and Masey opened the door to reveal

Derek and Cynthia, dressed to the nines, or perhaps that should be sixty-nines. Derek's ponytail looked even longer and silkier than I remembered, and Cynthia's dress even teensier than last time, but essentially, they hadn't changed. These were the beautiful people. And the beautiful people do not change. Just ask them.

They managed to all have some kind of group air-kiss, while doing as thorough a job of rubbing against, and feeling up each other as it's possible to do when two-thirds of the group are carrying large quantities of Thai food and scotch, and don't want to stain each other's clothes. Well, to be more truthful…when they don't want to stain each other's clothes just yet.

'You remember Wallace,' said Masey. 'Don't worry about the beard, it'll be going.'

'Wally,' I said. 'My name's Wally. And the beard will be staying. Get used to it.'

Derek tried to get his too-tight face to smile his warmest fake smile while shaking my hand with his warmest firmest I'm a real stand-up guy give me all your money shakedown handshake. Cynthia, knowing a smile was beyond her face's capabilities, batted her eyelashes in her own completely individual yet exactly the same as everyone else movie-star way, and managed to rub most of her body against mine as she kissed me full on the mouth with her fabulous freshly Botoxed lips.

'You look wonderful Wally,' she purred. At least, I think that's what she purred. It sounded too much like purring to be sure.

We ate our food. It was delicious. I didn't even know how much it cost, let alone whether they got any change. Everything felt different this time. I didn't need to drink. I didn't feel lost, or out of my depth, or like there was anything here to run away from. I let them enjoy their conversation, took part when and where it suited me, and kept myself totally under my own control.

When Cynthia tried to corner me in the kitchen, I made like Rudolph Valentino, or Rudolf Nureyev, or Rudolf the Red-nosed Raindog—whichever one was the alpha male type with the dark smouldering eyes—and ran my hand down her bare back, pulled her close, looked deep into her eyes and said in my best movie-star death-star porn-star voice, 'Not yet Cyn. I have something very special planned for you. Now behave yourself, and savour the anticipation. I know I am.'

The difference to last time fascinated me. Everything was different, yet everything was the same. Derek was the same, Cynthia was the same. Masey too, trying though she was to be different, was as self-absorbed and self-serving as ever. Which was fine. At least a man knew where he stood. The food was the same, the drink. The house was a little different, but not so much. *Smashing job Wally.* All that had really changed was me. Wallace was gone. I was Wally. Wally knew who he was. And Wally knew what he wanted.

When they couldn't take any more of the anticipation and the waiting, and something had to give, I ordered them to go upstairs and start without me. 'I'll be along a bit later,' I said. 'Don't worry about me, I'm preparing something special for us all. And look…'

I flipped open my laptop and showed them it was streaming live footage of our currently empty king-sized bed.

'…I have the room set up as a film studio. When you get there I'll start recording… and I'll be watching… Give it your all, my gorgeous young porn-stars. I'll join you all later.'

'Porn-stars,' they moaned breathily as one. Well, I think that's what they moaned breathily. It sounded too much like breathy moaning to be sure.

'Now, I know we're all keen to get started, but if we're going to be porn-stars we have to start acting responsibly,' I told them.

'Oh, not condoms?' whined Derek.

'Of course not,' I said. 'What's a little skin between friends? No, we all just have to sign some forms. So I can't get in any trouble for filming us. Otherwise it's no go, I'm afraid.'

'Yeah!' shouted Derek, thrusting his hips forcefully forward, presumably the fist-pump of the porn-star's world. 'Porn-star contract! Where do I sign?'

Derek quickly signed his as the girls read out the start of each page.

Cynthia signed next as they all jibber-jabbered excitedly.

Masey didn't even look at hers. She could have been signing her own death warrant and wouldn't have known or cared. The important thing was, that although none of my partners in porn had a solitary wrinkle around their eyes, they had a multitude of stars in them. All they could see with these bright starry eyes, was how they would one day be recognised for their services to porn-kind.

'Go to it, my pretties,' I said. 'And mark my words. This will be the most memorable twenty-four hours of our lives.'

'Twenty-four hours,' they gasped as one. Well, I think that's what they gasped. It sounded too much like gasping to be sure.

They rushed off to the bedroom, each no doubt determined to outshine the other with their wild sexual shenanigans. I watched them preen awhile, each of them working the camera, showing their best angles, contorting their plastic faces into the closest thing they could manage to smiles as they worked as a team to impress me, or the camera, or both. Or maybe I was wrong, maybe all they ever really wanted to impress was themselves. Then the strangest thing happened. After watching a few minutes, I felt a fondness for Masey that I realised had been missing a very long time. She was genuinely happy. I saw a joy in her there, as she postured for the camera and played and laughed with her friends. A joy I'd not seen in a really long time. Maybe not ever. And it wasn't just her — the others looked happy too. If it was enough for them, it was enough for me.

I closed the laptop, took out my phone and called James. The phone didn't do anything for a while, because sometimes that's what phones do when you're calling someone who's on the other side of the world. And then, just when I thought it wasn't going to work, which is the only time it does start to work, the phone went brrt brrt, brrt brrt, brrt brrt, brrt brrt, and my little boy, my darling baby boy, in his big deep grown-up engaged to another man voice, said, 'Hi Dad, Mum told me she was moving back home. Don't take any shit from her okay?' and I knew everything was going to work out just fine.

52
Wrapped

I SLEPT on the lounge in the cabana. It was a sleep only a truly happy man could sleep. I could get used to that, I'm pretty sure I thought. I awoke refreshed, hopeful of what the day might bring. Whichever way things went, I'd know I'd been alive. Isn't that the best shape sane can be?

I made coffee, bacon, sausages, eggs and burnt toast drowned in butter for myself and the porn-stars. Poor things were exhausted. Probably been waving bits of themselves at the camera most of the night. They were tired, hung over, a little disappointed I hadn't joined them before now, but appreciative of having breakfast made for them. It was a nice time. I felt close to them somehow. I told them to shower, shit, shampoo, to brush their teeth, but not to touch each other's bodies in a sexual way under any circumstances until I had everything prepared. Moisturising was compulsory. Nothing like rope biting into newly softened skin I'm told.

I made up the bed with clean white sheets. I had two rolls of duct tape — one red, one white. All my ropes, harnesses, slings, belay devices and carabiners were clean and at the ready. While they showered I attached slings to all the bedposts and at intervals across the bed-head, and looped ropes through the slings. All was as ready as I could make it until the soft glistening moisturised bodies returned from the showers. They returned naked and excited, together, but I was waiting outside the room with the door closed.

'One at a time,' I ordered. 'You first Big-Boy. My sexy, sexy ladies, wait downstairs. I'll call you.'

Two of Doctor Hung's finest middle-aged billboards walked downstairs, giggling like a pair of schoolgirls on Lebanese hash cookies.

I ushered Derek inside. 'Cool,' he said.

The scene was set, but for the three main props. This would be art, a gift to a discerning eye. Maybe I was an artist after all. No shit. Or maybe a little shit, who could know what the day would bring? The camera was above the door, looking down and into the room, the foot of the bed in the foreground.

I had Derek lie on the left side of the bed, close to the edge, but not so close he'd fall. We talked a little as I tied him tight. He was pleasant enough, not interesting, but co-operative. We worked together, got him comfortable, got the pillows just right under his head and knees.

'You'll be here awhile Derek. Might as well be comfy,' I explained.

When I was done, he lay on his back as still as a corpse, wearing only red leather underpants, and thanked me.

Then I taped his mouth so he couldn't speak. The red tape looked good on him I must say. I looked at the time. Right on schedule, I called Masey upstairs and let her into the room.

'Quite lovely, Wallace. When did you learn to make a bed?'

'Wally,' I said. 'My name's Wally. Now, my little nymphette. Put on your climbing harness then climb on top of Uncle Derek here and give him a nice lick all over his lovely clean face.'

She did as she was told. She was born to be a porn-star, but what she really needed was a good lesson in how to suck dick. And today, she'd be getting it.

'Off,' I said. 'Now, lie next to Derek facing away from him, that's it. Now shimmy your legs up the bed, and bend at the waist so your upper body runs parallel to the bed-head, and your legs stay parallel to Derek. Bit sharper bend at the waist my lovely. Very nice.'

'I am so fucking hot right now,' she said. 'Kiss me Wally.'

'Now now,' I said. 'Slaves don't tell slave-masters what to do. You'll be copping an extra lashing for that.'

'Promise?' she asked.

'Enough talk.' I taped her mouth with the lovely red duct tape, then tied her wrists tight with the white. Three minutes later, she was trussed and bound into place, unable even to squirm. She had become the top half of the number five, her face at the top edge of the bed — awaiting only the tearing off of the tape, so her mouth could be put to much better use than the endless complaining she'd used it for these past too-many-years. Her eyes looked directly across at the side wall, so I took advantage of the situation and wrote a message on the wall for her — OPEN WIDE — she couldn't speak with the duct tape still on, but her eyes seemed to like it.

I called Cynthia. She came running. Obedient. I was enjoying this more than I expected to. Cynthia looked at the bed, took in the colours, the art I'd been making. 'It's beautiful,' she said.

'Fifteen,' I said. 'It's a number you see, my flexible yoga-bodied hot baby. Now put on your harness and climb into place for your Uncle Wally.'

'Which way round?' she asked. 'God I want you to fuck me. That big cock. Fuck me now, in front of them both, before you tie me up.'

'Patience, my pretty,' I said. 'You'll be fucked soon enough. Head at Masey's feet, and twist into the best arc you can manage. That's it. Lovely easy access to your ... everything ... from the side of the bed here. Can you see the action well enough if I was to stand here and fuck Cynthia, Masey darling?'

Masey couldn't move anything except her eyes, but they were saying YES.

'Good view for you Derek?' I enquired. He eagerly nodded his head.

When I was done tying Cynthia, I stood back and surveyed my handiwork.

The colours were amazing. I, Wally Head, had created a thing of beauty. It almost gave me a hard Long Dong Silver. But not quite. The white of the sheets and the walls and the bed-head, the red of the harnesses and the duct tape, the purple and blue of the ropes and the slings. It seemed almost a sin to take the tape off their mouths, but I didn't have the heart to leave it on. At least then they'd be able to talk to each other while they awaited their fate.

I tore the tape from their mouths and checked every rope. I'd outdone myself. There would be no chance of escape. Bruce had taught me well.

Woof!

These three people, this living 15 adorning the bed, the beautiful people awaiting their director to say, "Action!" could barely move a muscle between them. Derek could turn his head. Masey could wiggle her feet and her fingers. Cynthia the same. And they couldn't touch each other, except for Cynthia being able to lick Masey's feet. It was as perfect as I could make it.

'Cynthia, there's a darling,' I said. 'Lick Masey's feet, will you?' And she did.

I checked the time. I really had to be going. 'Is everyone happy?' I asked.

'Yes,' they all said, and it was ever so clear, and sounded exactly like yes.

'I almost forgot,' I said. 'So beautifully wrapped, but no bow.' I went downstairs, found the huge red ribbon from the Tiny Police Force's very thoughtful gift, went back upstairs and tied a big perfect bow around Masey's feet and Cynthia's head.

'That's perfect, my little porn-stars, you look just beautiful,' I said. 'Now everyone relax and listen to Barry White. Don't worry darlings, the action begins in an hour. Don't do anything I wouldn't do. Oh, and do smile for the camera. I'll be watching…'

I turned up the music, walked out of the room, and left them yelling their little questions behind me.

53
Liquid Lightning

I CALLED BRUCE as I walked to my car. The phone went brrt brrt, brrt brrt, and Bruce went 'Wally, maaaate, how have you been? I've been worried about you mate. I'm so sorry about all the…'

'Bruce. Please be quiet and listen. I need you to do something for me.'

'Anything mate. Wally, it was a shit thing I did and I wanna…'

'Bruce, quiet. Meet me at my solicitor's office. It's in the same building as the Thai restaurant we go to. Upstairs. Number 21. Can you be there in five minutes?'

'Fair go Wally. Are you suing me or something? I…'

'Bruce. Just meet me there. Please. It's important.'

'No worries Wally. I'll be in my work clothes, is that alright mate?'

'That's perfect Bruce. See you there.'

Seven minutes later I was in the waiting room, and one minute after that Bruce was too. He was covered in sweat and grass clippings, and appeared to have dog-shit splattered on his legs.

'In the shit mate?' I asked him.

'Fucken dogs,' he said. 'Missed you Wally. Are ya suing me mate? I got nothing but my little place, you know that. And I…'

'Mister Head,' the receptionist said. 'Mister Vulture will see you now.'

'Let's go Bruce,' I said, screwing up my nose. 'You know, you could've washed that off mate.'

'I was walking to the hose when you called Wally. You said five minutes, so I threw the gear on the ute and drove like a maniac to get here on time. Shoulda fucken stayed there, all the appreciation I get.'

My solicitor and another man were in the room. Everyone introduced, we all took our seats.

'It's all done Mister Head, just as you asked. Everything's been paid for, and all the contracts drawn up. All that remains is for you to hand over the agreement you've had your wife sign, and all present to sign and date each documents on the desk here. We'll handle everything from there—but doing it this way, effectively the whole thing's done, airtight, locked up and can't be changed. Seems a very strange way of doing things, but it's not my job to tell you how to go about your business Mister Head. I'm sure you have your reasons.'

I looked at Bruce, and was pleased to see he had no understanding at all of what was going on.

'Let's sign some papers then shall we Bruce my friend?' I said.

'What fucken papers? Fuck Wally, what are you getting us into?'

The looks on the guys in the suits were priceless. I wished I'd thought to take photos. Instead, I took my laptop out of my bag.

'Can I have a minute please gentlemen?' I said.

They shook their heads like we were completely crazy, and my solicitor said, 'Call us when you're ready. I'm billing you by the hour, no matter what you do.' They walked out of the office and left Bruce and I alone.

'Bruce. Mate,' I said.

'What the fuck Wally? Are you completely nuts? What are you…'

'Bruce. Shut up. First, remember how you told me all that stuff about us not being crazy…'

'Clearly I was fucken wrong mate,' he said, 'but go on.'

'All that stuff about the shapes of sane, and you counted us all off, all fifteen of us, fifteen shapes of sane, remember that Bruce?'

'Yeah mate, I remember. But you should know better than to listen to me. I'm a dickhead and a loser. I fucked your wife and never told you. I'm a…'

'Bruce. Shut up mate. Look on the laptop here. This is what they call a live stream. I made it for you to celebrate.'

I showed him the laptop, with the live feed of my bed-room—the magnificent number 15 on the bed, ready and waiting for some enterprising fellow with a head full of dreams and a cock full of liquid lightning to turn up and ravage until you could no longer even tell what number it had been when he started.

'Fuck me Wally! Is that your missus? Who's the other two? Jeez, you'll get yourself fucken arrested mate. That's fucken brilliant.'

'That's Derek and Cynthia she ran away with. They all let me do it Bruce. Wanted me to. They even agreed to me filming it all. I have the signed documents here in my bag. Like the red ribbon tied in a bow mate?'

'Fucken nice bow mate, I'd swear a woman tied it. What's it all mean?'

'Present for you Bruce. You're the best friend I ever had. If it weren't for you I'd be stuck in a miserable marriage for the rest of my life. I'm out mate. I'm the happiest I've ever been. I know who I am Bruce, and I couldn't have done it without you.'

'Aw, mate, piss off,' he said. Then, looking at the screen again, 'Fuck mate, do they know I'm coming?'

'Not yet. They think it'll be me. I've got a red cape in my bag for you to wear when you get back there. Says SD on it, for SuperDick. On a picture of a huge pink pecker. They'll love it. Bruce, I'm not cut out for all that mad shagging, but they like it, and so do you. So I reckon we all need to swap our lives around a bit. Here. Look at these papers. This one lists everything we're signing.'

He read the list that summed it all up. He shook his head. He shook his head a lot. Clearly, being partners in a company that streamed real-life porn over the internet, and where the principals mowed lawns together three days a week had never occurred to him. 'I don't know nothing about film-making,' he said.

'You don't need to. I've got a bloke all organised to do that. He's gonna bring more cameras and set the place up better. Ex copper. You'll like him. Masey, Cyn and Derek are keen and signed up. They'll be getting a share in the profits to do what they love. You just live your life as normal, except you get all your new playmates to sign a release. The shy ones can wear masks if they want to. It's all here. Waddaya reckon Bruce?'

He got to the last item on the page. 'No way mate. No fucken way. We can't do this.'

'It's already done Bruce. It'll be a great earn for both of us, so it'll all work out right in the end. And you and me mow lawns, three days a week, two mates working together, or the whole deal's off, and I walk out of here and never speak to you again. Waddaya reckon Bruce?'

'I reckon the shape of your sanity's got a big fucken wobble in it mate. Yer fucken mad.'

'Take that as a yes then shall I Bruce?'

'Fuck me Wally. It's always the quiet ones ain't it? Get those suits back in here, and let's sign some papers mate.'

54
This Famous Flute

In the car park, I gave Bruce the keys, told him not to wash the dog-shit off because leaving it on would give the film added authenticity, and gave him a hug.

'Like a pair of gays already,' he said. 'Look at us. We musta caught it off that beaut kid of yours. Thanks Wally. I'll give you a wave when I get there.'

'Don't forget to put your cape on SuperDick,' I said.

He drove away smiling like a man who's just scored a million bucks, found his dream job, and got his best friend back.

I thought about my life. My friendships. My possibilities. There seemed so much possibility.

After a few minutes I opened the laptop to watch the action. The porn-stars were talking amongst themselves, wondering if their hour of waiting was almost over.

Suddenly the door flew open, and a madman in a flowing cape showing the letters SD on a large blue-veined custard-shooter burst into the room. The women screamed, and a fountain of bright yellow pee made a perfect arc above Derek's little wiener.

'G'day me lovelies,' said Bruce. 'Who's ready for some stretching exercises, courtesy of SuperDick?'

The girls laughed, Derek informed everyone he nearly shit himself, Bruce turned to the camera to give me a big thumbs up before heading around to teach Masey a lesson — and I closed the laptop on that part of my life for the very last time.

I took out my phone and called Tess. The phone went brrt brrt, brrt brrt, brrt brrt, brrt brrt, brrt brrt, brrt brrt, brrt brrt, brrt brrt, and just when I thought she'd decided never to answer my calls again, a surprisingly powerful-sounding voice said, 'Therese ... Speak.'

'Ummm. Hi Tess, it's Wally.'

'Ah, Wally,' she said. She sounded happy. It was going better than I'd expected. 'You were fantastic last night. You left your pink fluffy handcuffs at my place, by the way.'

'I ... I ...'

'Is there a problem Wally?'

'I ... I mean, I'm Wally Head, remember? Not ... Who do you ...'

'Just pulling your leg Wally. Not getting any quicker are you? Of course I remember you. How could I forget? Tall guy. Rubber mask. Married to a woman who walks around armed with a whirring dildo with its own spinning finger. Yes Wally, how can I help you?'

'Well Tess, I ...'

'Yes Wally? Let me guess. You're calling everyone you know to see if they wish to participate in the next Sexual Olympics? I suppose I could start training. I hear there are plenty of men on the internet looking for training partners.'

'Tess?'

'Yes Wally?'

'Well, I just wanted to tell you Tess, I don't live with Masey anymore. I moved out this morning.'

'Throw you out did she? Don't worry, she'll take you back Wally. Nice girl like her. Wear your mask, she'll think you're somebody else.'

'Well, actually Tess, she doesn't know yet. But she's about to find out. There's been a few changes. Quite a few in fact.'

'Oh yes? How so?'

'Well, I sold my half of the house. Swapped it actually. You know that little mud-brick place? The one in the bush at the end of the lane? It's mine now. Clean swap with my friend Bruce.'

'Ah. So you're insane then? Your place is worth, what? Six times what that place is? Why would you do that?'

'Because money's just money Tess. Because what's in our hearts matters more than what's in our bank accounts. Because I listened to what you said, and went looking for myself—and when I found me, I realised I was living the wrong life. So I swapped the bits of it that weren't working for some bits that might.'

'Hmmm. Maybe you're not as crazy as I thought Wally Head. So why are you telling me all this?'

'I'll tell you Tess, but first, will you answer one question for me?'

'Ask the question and find out Wally. Never know your luck I suppose.'

'Why did you come around on Thursday? I thought you didn't like me any more. You said I was just a liar and a sleaze with a purple rope.'

'Okay Wally, I was wrong. Rosemary came over to my house. She was telling me how useless you were. How you knocked yourself unconscious trying to escape when she and her friend tried to have a threesome with you. She told me several things in fact, most of which were too much information, and don't bear repeating. But I am sorry. Satisfied? So again, why are you telling me all this?'

'Well, last night I spoke to my son. He's a great kid, wise beyond his years too. He's getting married soon you know. And I told him I might be crazy. That I was leaving his mother, and was swapping my half of the house for a place I love that's worth a fraction of what mine is. And he said, "About time, Dad. Go and be happy. It's the best thing for you, and for mum too I reckon." I told you he was smart didn't I?'

'Yes you did. And?'

'And I told him that wasn't the crazy part. I told him I'm in love with a woman I've only known a few weeks, and that I'm hoping she'll be crazy enough to want to be with me too. And that I'm planning on spending the rest of my life with her, or at least giving it a red hot go — even though she's the jealous type, and has been known to jump to conclusions and get cranky for no reason sometimes.'

'Hmmm. And what did this wise son of yours have to say about that Wally?'

'He said, "It's not crazy Dad. Not if it's really love. Sounds to me like you've finally found yourself. And if Who You Are thinks it's love, Who You Are is probably right. And if you're wrong, you'll pick yourself up and dust yourself off and try again. That's life Dad. It's your life. So live it." ... That's what he said.'

'Smart kid. I like him already.'

'I love you Tess. I think you're just beautiful. I know it's a lot to take in and a lot to consider, and I know I'm a difficult person at times, but aren't we all? Anyway, I've told you, so now you know. I'm going home now, and that's where I'll be most of the time for a while, except for when I'm out mowing lawns every Tuesday, Wednesday and Friday. If you wanna come see me, you know where I am.'

Free Review Copies

If you enjoyed this story, please consider spending a minute of your time rating the book and posting a short review somewhere.

Honest book reviews are a great help to us all, readers and writers alike, and when you write one you perform a valuable service.

For a free copy of one of our other books to review, please go to silkyoakpress.com.au and request the book that interests you.

We give away 25 copies of each of our books in exchange for honest reviews.

Whether you're a professional reviewer, a book blogger, or a reader who's happy to write an honest review, your opinion is important.

You'll also find some great author interviews, interesting articles, even some wonderful stories you won't find anywhere else, including a few you can listen to. Who wouldn't want to hear a bedtime story, read to them by their favourite author?

So come on over — we'd love to hear from you.

'Well thank you Wally. That really is a very interesting offer my friend... Tell you what. It's a little quiet here today. I suppose I could come over and meet you for a housewarming drink in, shall we say, two hours? And Wally...'

'Yes Tess?' I asked, barely able to breathe with excitement as my new life unfolded before me.

'I'll pick up some extra large condoms on the way, and we'll see how big this famous flute of yours really is.'

'I... umm, I... Ah Tess, you're just pulling my leg again. Aren't you?... Tess?... Tess?'

And the phone went...

— THE END —

About the Author

Harry Pants is the pseudonym of someone who probably should know better. He is definitely not the lovechild of Jane Austen and Chuck Palahniuk.

Feel quite free to complain about this book to him at harryipants.wordpress.com but please don't tell him that Midlife is a romance novel. He thinks it's literary fiction, and is expecting a call from the Man Booker prize judges anytime soon.

Silky Oak Press
— books that love you back

Nice words, but what do they mean? Obviously, good books need great writing, editing and proofreading. Our standards are as high as any in the industry. But more than that, we believe a book should be a thing of beauty, with beautiful typography, gorgeous cover art, and nary a typo to be found. We take pride in our work, and will do whatever it takes to create books you'll love — books so good, it's like they love you back.

— Other Books Out Now —

White by Conrad Jaymes

Conrad Jaymes takes us into the darkest corners of the drug war and introduces us to some of her combatants. Peter Balino: a tough, complex man, haunted by his past, unsure of his future. The Say Tong: the most powerful criminal organisation in East Asia, run by men of knife-edge ambition and cruelty. Men known as Snake Eyes, The Vampire and The Giant.

This is a story for fans of true crime. A story born in the headlines. A story so real it may just be true.

The Ballad of Sergeant Collins by Conrad Jaymes

You've heard it said: they don't make cops like they used to. Well, they never made another like Sergeant Collins. Legend? Maverick? A force of his own. These are some of his stories.

Aiden's Alibi by D.B. Allen

A year into mourning his wife, James Davison still wonders how to move on. Could Aiden's mother be the answer, or just another question. This brilliant contemporary story of love, lust and loss is Book One in D.B Allen's Relationships Series.

Coming Soon

The Rainbow Blindness by D.B. Allen

Heart Land by D.B. Allen

Silver by Conrad Jaymes